THE HOLY SPIRIT DANCE CLUB

By Joseph Puccia

LIBERTY PRESS

For my parents

Welcome to the Pleasure Dome.
-Frankie Goes To Hollywood

May The Force be with you.
-Luke Skywalker

TABLE OF CONTENTS

This secret place

It wasn't the first year the Club opened, the year John Lennon was killed and a sniper shot into a crowd at the Ramrod. That first year forty-four Americans were hostage in Iran and the country was on the precipice of a conservative swing backward as we enjoyed the last few minutes at a height of liberalism. That was when Robert and I heard all about this new Club that would put every other club out of business. Crisco Disco was still open and there were bag transvestites on West Street. That was the year Robert and I were still dancing at 12 West, the clone club near the Hudson River, or taking mescaline and hanging out in the Anvil, the synthasleazy after-hours on the truly seamy triangle at 14th Street and 12th Avenue.

There were good drag shows there and I guess we saw the end of the culture that'd preceded us. That was the year you could still see emaciated boys dancing for drugs on the bar, before and after shows featuring Ruby Rims or the Amazing Yuba, who did a great Grace Jones and an acid-ized delineation of "Hey, Big Spender." And there was one other wispy, straggly blond who looked like a heroin addict propped up against the wall who sang a lot of Deborah Harry and something like "D Is For Getting A Divorce."

During the Club's second year there was still something to do every night of the week and

1

Robert and I, taking the subway in from Brooklyn and meeting under Village Cigars, always had a round of bars to go to every night except Monday. We ran from bar to bar and day to night, the movements an arcane knowledge available to anyone who wanted to join and could learn the itinerary. That's when Christopher Street was a garden party on Sunday afternoons and it was the last summer the Ice Palace on Fire Island was any good. A major gay gym opened on the circuit and Radio City got saved and premiered a movie called *Escape from New York*. Donna Summer was over that year, *Torch Song Trilogy* opened uptown, and 12 West closed. And that was my first awareness that things could change.

Barishnykov was still dancing and Lynn Taylor Corbett was a new choreographer then. *Sunday in the Park with George* opened on Broadway, unemployment was some bizarre percent and I lost my first job; I mean like, I lost a job for the first of what'd be some number of times.

This story is about the Club's third season, the year it peaked because after that it fell. This is when things were just beginning to change: the year before the beginning of the end of New York City, the year before several thousand men were missing, the year before any of us knew what a rubber looked like. Before the Anvil, the Mineshaft and the baths closed. Before people started doing whatever the fuck they're doing now (as I sit here writing since I have nothing else to do; but it's what The Holy Spirit Dance Club gave me), which is probably nothing. It was a time when we could be as flagrant as we enjoyed and yet our fraternity was a secret club. It was the last year of hardcore disco, when you could still

2

go into the Club and see people doing things you never knew people did.

This is when Bundingswear tank tops made their forbidding appearance and anything Japanese was big. Madonna's first movie was *Desperately Seeking Susan* while East Village Art got termed and classified. This is about the group who came after the clones and the guys who were in charge during the first couple of years. It's about the group of us who presided over the last days of the circuit, during the last and loudest beat of liberal lifestyles and an ethic of pleasure.

There were a few women on the circuit by this time as disco became more eclectic than it ever was before. These few women evidently eschewed traditional lesbian company and were more like queens than dykes; I think they probably had been queens in previous lives. The effect being, The Holy Spirit was more differentiated than it'd been the last time I was there, more than a year earlier, and there were different types of people out by this time. OK, to a certain extent. It was clones, the guys who'd been dancing a long time who were around long before I ever made it into a disco, and it was also younger boys, some lesbians, and a few people like me from the Lower East Side.

It was second generation disco, a year when some of the men started to disappear, when the ranks thinned just a little, when the clones didn't predominate anymore. It was a year of pedal pushers and pajamas, and it was a year boys tucked 501s into their high tops and went dancing. A new group was in charge.

And this is about a Club that had a code of behavior: like if you acted out, you got a letter from management. Members had to phone in guests or arrive with them, and you were responsible for your guests' actions. You'd also get a letter if other members wrote and complained over any inappropriate behavior or some kind of breach on the dance floor. There was a nurse's office. The Club opened at midnight, since we were outlaws, and the music stopped around noon. Parties went till two p.m. except the White Party which closed at five and a New Year's that went on for two days. (There was a break in between.) Every season closed with a Closing Party and then they opened again.

T/Vs were really outlawed and dresses were not allowed except in the case of gender fuck. Sneakers were required, heels were prohibited for the few women, there was no smoking on the dance floor. Your social affiliation was where you danced and who you got your drugs from. No photographic equipment was permitted inside the Club. If anyone o.d.'d, it was rumored, the body was quietly removed; I heard a story about two guys who carried their friend around for hours after he died. I heard another story about someone's ashes scattered over the dance floor.

From that September to the next June the high energy songs were "Electric Dreams" and "Never Ending Story," two versions of "My Heart's On Fire," "False Alarm," "Girl Of The 80's," "Coming Out Of Hiding" and "You Make My Heart Beat Faster (And That's All That Matters)." Sleaze, the morning music, was "Tonight," "Guardian Angel," Tina Turner singing "What's Love Got To Do With It?" "Islands In The Stream" by Dolly Par-

4

ton, Paul Young's "Love Of The Common People," and "I Just Called To Say I Love You." These songs were exciting and personal, and we rushed upstairs to dance to every one of them. And only sometimes, there was the excitement of hearing a song you'd never heard before but it was your song, one that worked you from its first upbeat.

The music started to change and we heard "Forever Young" by Alphaville, who also did "Big In Japan," and Robin Gibb did "Boys Do Fall In Love" as things got rocker. The dance floor looked like an enchanted sparkling room under these songs. This was during the emergence of Bronski Beat and their *Age of Consent* album with the pink triangle on the cover and "Small Town Boy" on the vinyl. The Eurythmics made "Would I Lie To You?"; the Police did "Every Breath You Take"; and Men Without Hats made "Where Do The Boys Go?" and "Rhythm Of You." Tastes in music created factions and hating someone else's favorite song could start an argument; at the least it generated attitude. A bad night at the Club could ruin your week. You never made any other plans for the weekend. You never scheduled anything important for Monday. And something else: there was this undertone that we all knew we were going to make it; we knew we'd be the high achievers of our generation, and the songs had this surge of affirmation in them.

One of the best things about the Club and about our lives on the circuit at that time was, it was all a secret. The world, our families and the people we worked with, all had no idea. Maybe if we let slip something about dancing till four p.m. or live snake shows they'd be surprised; but they had no idea. And we never mentioned the name of the Club and the media never heard of it. There was no sign or marquee outside and it was a secret. Cabdrivers didn't know about it and never lined up in the street in the morning; even to other members, we never mentioned its name outside the Club's walls. It was always "the Club" or, "Are you going out this weekend?" It wasn't even written on our membership cards.

This secrecy, then, made it a metaphor since what was going on inside the Club was a secret too, even to some of the people who went there all the time. Consider the selection process: first, that only a small part of the population even knew about the place. Second, that within that small portion only a subgroup of that ten percent ever came there. And of all the people who did, only some came again and often, becoming members. It was a culling process.

I for one definitely got culled, rough. I went there the first year it opened, once, and I blacked out and left and didn't come back until the second year. That time I had a bad trip and ran, almost pushed, my way out, caught the subway to Brooklyn and didn't come back until the Club's third year. The point being that things happen to people when they're ready for them to happen.

So that's me, Harold Fenestere; that's with a long e on the end. Also that's pronounced thuh end not thee end since I have recently forsaken everything I learned about being assimilated. I never used to have a Brooklyn accent at all until around a few years ago when I got this job with a real patrician organization, at which point I found out I was non-white.

What I am, and I won't be so disingenuous as to pretend I'm demographically unclassifiable, is twenty-seven years old and living on East Eleventh Street and Avenue B. Sometimes working, otherwise collecting, depending on how well I'm relating to the power structure at a given moment. I have by this time understood that it's all about the man, and further figured out, not too swiftly since it's taken twenty-seven years, that I am not the man. Which is the way I prefer it.

By this time also, I'm not trying to fit in anymore, like when I made my first attempts in The Dance Club; by this time I'm figuring it's OK to be on the outside, politically and socio-economically. And in case anyone can't figure it out right away, that's why I moved to the Lower East Side and got wire rimmed spectacles. And for anyone who still doesn't get it, that's why I wore ripped and torn T-shirts and never got out of sneakers and 501s. But anyway, I don't mean to sound too cocky, since I definitely was not that self-assured when all this started. It's just that I was definitely that way by the time it was over.

One more introduction, my friend Robert, the one who travelled the bars and the circuit with me. Apparently he was ready for The Holy Spirit before I was because he became a member and brought me there. But I resisted and when I finally agreed to go to this Club again where I'd been overwhelmed twice already, Robert just put me on the guest list and said, I'll see you there. That's important, because one thing I've learned is that each movement has to come from inside; you've got to do it yourself. That's dancing.

Robert, you should know, is Italian and Jewish. He like grew up in Bensonhurst; something

I was spared by more catholic parents. We met when we were seventeen (ten years ago) and we were busboys at Dubrow's on Kings Highway in Brooklyn. I worked there part time after college while he worked there full time after dropping out of high school. This co-worker who came to work on no sleep and got mysterious phone calls all day intrigued me and I saw this route to a whole other life. "Who was that?" I asked him.

"A friend," he said and smiled at his own mysteriousness as he continued cleaning a table. He had these large features and he looked strong. His thick hair fell over his forehead as we worked.

"A friend from where?" I asked. "Or would you rather not say?"

"I have no problem saying," he said. "I just don't think the answer is half as interesting as you imagine. I think you're the type of person who makes a big deal out of things."

"That's very analytical for a busboy," I said.

"Yeah, ain't it," he said.

"I guess you think I'm being nosy," I said. I put my hands in my pockets.

"I think you're a Poindexter," he said. "And I think you're being, what was your word, analyzing. And we're cleaning tables."

I got the point, for the time being, but later I tried again. "Well, when do you go to these places?" I asked another time when he finally gave me some details.

"We're going out tonight," he said. "You can come if you want." And I did. He showed me the life of the not-college-bound and people who stayed up all night and ran all over town; I was fascinated. But that was ten years ago; the point being, Robert was in at the beginning of this story. He was the one responsible for both of us being in The Holy Spirit Dance Club at all, and you can be sure he's taking full credit for everything that happened.

Inside the Club

On a cool black night at the end of September I approached the Club. I stood there in glasses and my torn jeans and a ripped black T-shirt. It was the season's first night.

"Yes?" the seriously delineated clone asked stentoriously. The outline of his dark, short hair ran through his stolid stance at the podium.

"I'm on the guest list," I said.

"Over there," he nodded.

I walked over to the window he nodded to, which I guessed used to be the ticket booth when this place was a concert hall.

"Fenestere," I said to the queen behind the counter. There was a dim light shining on him, like I was approaching a grotto.

"'Harold?'" he read from the card he pulled from his guest file.

"Yes," I said gratefully, and took the paper he handed me. I noticed Robert's name on the bottom of the sheet; probably since I was his guest. He was responsible for me. I thought of the letter he told me he got one week after one of his guests had to be carried to the nurse's office.

"To your right," the guy said, indicating the massive doors. "Have fun," he smiled.

"Thanks," I said, turning to the doors without falling over.

I entered a large empty chamber. At an elevated marble desk sat another queen, another well-built, short-haired young man. I felt like I was approaching a high official in a communist country for a favor. I handed him my guest papers. He wrote on the top sheet, tore out a carbon, and slid it back over the marble counter.

I passed through to the next room, where there was another marble counter, and presented my papers again.

"Twenty dollars," the queen said, and I gave him my money.

Finally I entered the Club. By this time I didn't know where I was. I mean, I knew where I was address-wise, but the enormity of the place made all geography meaningless.

I walked into the bar area, down some steps into an area as high as it was wide: a dark coliseum. Everything was gray, black and with a touch of red from the exotic flower arrangement on the bar.

The high-tech bar where no liquor was served was in the middle, with the crowd surging outward hive-live. Thousands of men moved in and out, talking and moving playfully, and you could hear the driving disco beat in the background coming from upstairs— "Megatron Man" working excitedly and electronically in these semiconductor times.

Paranoiacally I wondered if anyone knew that I was new there, but evidently I fit in; the place accepted me. It didn't ask any questions. Like, why did you major in that? Or, where do you want to be in five years? All the disco asked was that you be interesting and goodlooking.

"There you are," Robert said as if he'd been looking for me. He stood next to me.

"Huh?" I asked.

"I have," he said, skipping over a part of the conversation, or just implying the syntactic completion of some tense, which I think is allowed in Bensonhurst. "I've been looking for you," he insisted.

"Well," I said, standing at the steps below the dance floor.

"What are you doing here?" he asked me.

I just looked at him. I opened my mouth to answer and he handed me a capsule; I swallowed it. "What was it?" I asked, propitiated.

"MDA," he said.

"Oh, right," I said. "That drug you were telling me about. Tell me again what it does."

"You'll see," he said. He cleared his throat. "I'll be back," he said walking away. "I'm working on being a mess," he called back.

I stood there and looked at it all: shirtless men in jeans and boys in walking shorts went past me. They seemed very happy and I was sure this was a good place to be. I followed them up the stairs and up more stairs and through the darkness and I was on the dance floor.

The dance floor

And I passed through this portal entrance at twelve o'clock (twelve o'clock because it was the one near the d.j. booth) and it was like stepping into the tv screen: what I was looking up at climbing the stairs was all around me and it was moving and I moved in with it. The accelerating intro beats of "My Heart's On Fire" drew me in.

Everyone was intent on what they were doing in this mad scene and they looked more like specialized creatures than people. Some were travelling two at a time, their hips moving first from one side and then from the other, making a remarkable progress. There were boys in boxer shorts and pajama bottoms and high top sneakers and they danced like agitated flowers as the lights flashed around them. And there were signs of unity on the dance floor, these nouveau boys dancing next to clone contingents, whose bodies stayed in one place, their black Patrick feet on the ground where their bodies worked furiously upward through their 501's. Some of them played tambourines, others had rags hanging from their mouths, and all their T-shirts were moving from their hips at their belt loops.

Dancing in I moved into the places vacated by the other dancers' shifting movements. Every spot on the dance floor was taken and used in every moment. Sleek, beautiful guys in black jeans and boots and no shirts rocking crazily upwards were black elegant birds fluttering madly on the surface. I looked around and I saw groups of men dancing in circles of threes and fours. They were carrying on, acting out, sweating and screaming, and turning around in little circles and walking up to each other and walking away quickly. When I didn't see tambourines I heard them, also handbells and castanets. I looked around again and I saw one group cloaked in white sheets: the ones with the handbells. One of them had a round wooden thing that gyrated and made a grinding noise. They looked like jungle creatures assembled for a ritual, wild and secret.

And more groups: Orange People, thin men with moustaches all dressed in the same color, T-shirts and painter's pants. Fan dancers, more thin men moving quickly, flourishing their silver fans upwards and down like wings and I thought about the imagery of Daedalus and Stephen Daedalus occurring there.

I couldn't even tell where I was anymore. I danced in and moved and gyrated and travelled and we all moved like one being and I began to get the idea of a composite something bigger than all its parts together. The beat went faster and as we danced we moved faster and faster, with a velocity like running. I was smiling broadly from the speed and I was extraordinarily happy, experiencing pure joy. How could we be going so fast? But it was the speed and as each person went faster it affected another dancer, and the pace of the whole large being cranked up this way. We were going faster than ourselves, and by that I mean we were going faster than we could've if we thought about it. Don't think; move.

A happy man next to me pulled his rag from his mouth and handed it to me with a bottle and I sprayed the rag and stuck it in my mouth. The lights flashed, maybe in my head or maybe on the dance floor, and I looked up and something conceptual was wafting back and forth between two positions, and the idea laughed at me but in a friendly way. "What are you worrying about?" I understood it saying to me. "Everything's all the same anyway," it communicated. It was a simple address to a paranoid self-consciousness but later it began to mean other things to me. I don't know if this thought came to me, like in figuring something out or if I was directly addressed because it came in complete sentences. It was revelation, I figured, in the middle of this madness. I looked around at all the people acting out and if this dancing was primitive, then it could be revelation. Anyway, this is what I thought that night and this is how I started to believe The Holy Spirit was a sacred spot.

Then just when I was thinking it was maybe, like, something jungle or something primitive, an army sergeant, big and strong looking with a grey beard stubble and definitely a sign of civilization, danced by. I handed back the rag and the bottle as I danced, nodding my thanks. The duality I just saw resolved on the ceiling expressed itself to me as a backwards and forwards and I translated that into the positive and negative components of the basic unit of life. I saw the dancers around me dancing back and forth at each other, one trying to reach the other, the other eluding his pursuer, then the roles changing. I thought about sex, I thought about male and female and yin and yang. "It's all the same anyway." If I was being taught a basic duality, how was this happening in the disco? What a secret this place is, I thought, and looked around me at all these other men who led regular lives during the week, and no one had any idea they came to this mega-Club for a primitive ritual. Then the disco ball came out of the ceiling.

I noticed a young brown-haired woman, dressed in jeans and a T-shirt to underplay her beauty, raise her arms as the ball came down. She was the center of a group of boys and they all imitated her motion, raising their arms to hail the mirror ball. The music built up to a high point and we were all drenched as we moved around and kept moving. But dancers were looking up as they danced and the music was breaking and the opening choruses of "Tell Me Why" repeated their scream.

Everyone screamed and cheered as the introductory choruses gave way to the opening of the song and the ball settled into its place over the dance floor. It hung directly over the center of the floor, over the running and travelling. All the groups kept moving, chasing and eluding as if the appearance of the ball was the reason for it all. It was an object of worship.

And then out of the center of the dance floor, a hydraulic steel tree grew upwards as its arms grandly unfolded and spread its steel arms over the inner circle of the dance floor. It projected lavender, blue and yellow lights from its branches and they projected through the hazy steam of the energy that was rising over the floor.

And on top of the tree a huge black oval machine rotated, covered with tiny spots all over. I looked up and I realized that it wasn't an

16

irregular pattern. This star machine projected the universe onto the steel canvas of the dance floor's ceiling, a perfectly arced dome, and it was like dancing in black night on a mountaintop at the highest point of the world. I thought I was in a wilderness clearing where all these special people were gathered.

I looked up and watched the delegations walking on and off the dance floor, different contingents streaming past me. A group of muscle men marched by and then another group that looked pretty much the same, only shot down about twenty percent. I looked around and the room flashed black and white like the thunderous music, and for just a moment the context of the room changed. It looked square instead of round, there was space among the dancers where I hadn't seen it before, and the movement and the colors of the room changed. We were somewhere else, but someplace familiar even if we had never been there before. And then the lights flashed again and we were back in all the darkness and it was the first scene again.

A single white light projected from the star machine and circumnavigated the dance floor: a Japanese woman appeared next to me dancing frenetically, turning around nucleically in her group. One guy danced into the middle with her; they danced together while the others danced around the sides. Another guy danced kneeling before her and waved his fan. They danced low on the floor and then, as they came up, she looked at me and winked. Then her attention immediately folded back in on her friends.

In all these groups and travelling individuals, acting out and moving around, people were dancing alone and with each other, changing affiliations as the movement called for it. This was incredible madness occurring in this building, and from the outside of it you'd pass by and never know what was going on inside.

I had the feeling that at any moment everyone was going to laugh at me and tell me it was all a big joke and maybe say something like, "You mean you thought we were serious?" Doubt is fatal and I decelerated abruptly. The steam on the dance floor was going up as I was coming down and I walked over to the sidelines, to the banquettes surrounding the perimeter of this oval and leaned against their first level. I ran my fingers through my hair and shook the sweat from my head. I was soaked as I leaned there, watching some of the others, carrying on and running past in culottes, riding pants and Dr. Dentons. I stood back as two boys in white ice cream vendor's pants walked past me. Before they sat down they switched their T-shirts hanging from their back belt loops like white animals shaking their tails. By the outskirts of the dance floor a tall man playing the wooden sticks and dressed in khaki pants propelled up in the air beside me. I leaned there cooling off, watching the energy rise in a steaming mass. I'd never seen the tangible physical output of human exertion concentrated in an enclosed space before. Then I understood how something primitive could be happening there. It was designed for it. It was in the movements of the dancers and how they affected each other until cultural contingents had sprung up on the dance floor, adjoining to those adjacent. The Holy Spirit cohered into one group: basic nature.

18

The dancers moved back and forth at each other in a charged effort for balance: I thought it was the basic duality. I understood finally about positive and negative, about the interaction that binds all units in couples, growing outward into clusters. I thought about ions, zygotes and heartbeats and I understood there that everything works in contention for resolution: back and forth. My mind was racing from speed and acid, I'd lost track of what I'd taken and I thought insanely about a two party system, about conversational banter, the United States and the U.S.S.R., tennis and sex.

It was in the music, too, and the d.j. was the high priest of this art. It was in the way that he started with slow building music and then worked his way up to faster songs and higher energy until he peaked it at that moment of the ball's appearance. If that was the height then it preceded the beauty of descent as the music slowed a bit, but this bit lasted for hours as I watched dancers still happily affecting each other and creating the larger being on the dance floor. And then the music slowed into Sleaze. By now it was six a.m. and the music broke: there was lightning across the dome and it reverberated in overwhelming metallic musical strains as we brought in the absolute madness of the countdown to destruction from Two Tribes and you couldn't doubt any more the ultimate significance of the place and the auspicious activity there.

The dome, huh? Yeah, I thought. This was the world alright.

A living archetype

Which is what I said to Tom Sanders when the subject of the dome came up. I said, "Yeah. Some 'dome.' I like their sense of metaphor here."

Tom snickered, and he turned to Robert. "Aren't you going to introduce me to your friend?" he asked in an attenuated drawl. I remembered Robert telling me Tom was from Texas.

Robert cleared his throat before going on with this. "Harold," he said, "this is Tom." Tom stuck out his hand. He was wearing a tight black nylon sweatsuit with a white stripe up the side, so the first thing I inferred about him was, he must like extremes and court dichotomy. This was a friend of Robert's?

Tom still had his hand out. He looked like a creature extending something disgusting he wanted me to confront. Hallucinogenic powder was pumping through my veins as fast as my blood was speeding through my body and I was conscious of everyone in the room being wired. "Pleased to meet you, " I said and I took in the long black hair, his pearly black eyes, the "I love New York" T-shirt. His eyes had the look of someone who knows what you're thinking and thinks it's funny.

I thought it must be some in-born trait, that look. I held his glance, and I thought his black metal eyes were laughing at me. "What are you thinking, Harold?" he asked me.

"I was just thinking," I informed him, "that you're the doctor who performs autopsies for a living and I'm wondering if that means you have some clinical interest in all this."

Robert was horrified and he laughed uncertainly but Tom laughed and clapped his hands. That infuriated me. "What else gives you that impression?" he asked me. "I mean, do you have another point to draw that line through?"

"Well, actually, I do," I said putting my hands in my pockets. I knew I was performing at his command but I was enjoying myself anyway. Robert never let me speak this frankly. "I figure your T-shirt is a pretty bare admission that you're here for the show."

"Isn't it fabulous?" he asked. "I'm so glad you noticed it."

"Now who could miss reading your opinion of all this written across your chest? We're glad you like us."

"And I'm glad to be here," he said.

"Yeah," Robert put in. "Tom was just telling me that before he came to New York he thought people like me were just on television."

I was appalled. We sat down against the wall. "So do you live in Brooklyn, too?" he asked me.

"No," I said. "I was born in Brooklyn, and I've lived in various parts of it. But now I live on East Eleventh Street."

"So you were born in Brooklyn," he repeated, and I turned and looked at Robert.

"Did you ever live in Bensonhurst, like Robert?" he asked.

"No," I said. "And anyway, I don't obsess about Brooklyn. I couldn't wait to move," I added, realizing too late I was reacting obviously.

21

Tom Sanders laughed at my frankness. I knew this wasn't just in my head. He took a bottle out of his pocket and spooned out some powder and held it under Robert's nose. Without even looking down at it, Robert flared the corner of his nostril and the powder went up in a vacuum.

Then Tom repeated the procedure with me and I did my best to appear like Robert and get the powder to just ascend my nostril. Then Tom did some himself.

Robert stood up. He snorted once more, I guess a signal of thanks. "Well, I'll see youse," he said. I nodded that it was OK to leave me with this creature. He smiled blankly from his drugs and took off.

"'Youse,' I love that," Tom said. Actually what he said was more like, "Ah luv that." He had a heavy Southern accent. "'Youse,'" he said again, and shook his head. "I just love that," he said. "That's what I came to New York for."

"Me too," I said. "That's why I moved to Manhattan, to get away from people who talk like that. Not that anyone talks that way in the part of Brooklyn I come from," I added.

"That's too bad," Tom said. "I think that's fabulous. I love Robert. He tries so hard to pretend that everything's just what it looks like."

"What do you mean?" I asked.

"I mean," he said, "that Robert evidently comes from a part of Brooklyn that I honestly thought was just made up for television. He comes from a background where you don't assess anything existential and yet he can't help it. He's been cursed with an awareness that you can evaluate things and it's created a conflict for him." His thin moustache twitched; then he leered.

"So I was right," I said. "You did come to New York to observe the lifeforms here as clinically as you perform your job."

"What's wrong with that?" he asked.

"I'm not sure," I said. "But clinical detachment is suspect, I think. And certainly if you're going to come here to observe, you can't object to your specimens expressing their own objections, at the very least."

"No," he said. "I guess you can object as much as you want, though I don't know why the idea of wriggling in a petri dish like some one-celled unit of struggling life should bother you."

I laughed. "I just wanted you to know that someone is watching you. And we're going to pull you into the little glass dish with us. But listen," I said. "Let me ask you a question."

"I'm afraid," he laughed. "After all the declarative statements I've just listened to from you, I'm not sure if I can handle an interrogative one."

"Oh, that's just the drugs," I said. "Since last season I've been listening to Robert tell me all these bizarre things that go on here and then he adds it all up and he thinks it's the drugs."

"Ah know," he said. "That's almost as good as when he said before that I thought people like him were just on television. He knew what he was saying. But what do you think it is?"

"I think it's real life. I have this feeling that everything we're experiencing here is actually happening and that everything I saw up on that dance floor—you know, the subtext-type stuff— is really going on. I don't think drugs make things up, I think everything I saw up there is too

related to the basic structure of life to be ficti-
tious."

"I agree," he said. "Drugs don't distort reality.
They amplify it."

"So you know what I'm talking about," I said.

"I'm afraid that I do," he laughed. "But I can't
believe that you're actually talking about it," he
said turning sideways to look at me.

"Why not?" I asked. "You aren't hesitant
about your clinical approach to us as lifeforms.
So let me ask you that question: what exactly is
going on up there?"

"Girl," he drawled, "your guess is as good as
mine."

"Did you notice," I asked, "some feeling that
everyone is, like, cooperating?"

"That's a good term for it," he said. "Here," he
said. "Let's do more MDA."

I knew we didn't need any more because it's
supposed to last like eight hours and my nerves
were jumping up and down. But I snorted some
and handed the bottle to him. He knocked some
out on his fist and then inhaled it in that giant
vacuum again, that exaggerated gross gesture
that I couldn't help but interpret as a love of
overstatement and maybe even rudeness. That
would be consistent with his choice of occupa-
tion, anyway. "Listen," I said. "Something is going on up there. I feel like everyone is cooperating in some project. I mean, they have this look
on their faces, like they all know the same thing."

"What do you think it might be?" he asked me.

"I'm not sure, but there's something else I noticed, too. Did you get that feeling up there that
there's some way to resolve apparently opposed
forces?"

"I can't believe you're talking about this."

"But do you know what I'm talking about?"

"Well, of course I do, I've had that feeling up there too. But it *is* the drugs," he added.

"I'm not sure," I said. "I have this theory that there's something going on up there on the dance floor, something we're building up to, and something to be resolved. And just for mentioning it at all, I think I have some role in it. And because you are who you are, I think you have the other important role. There are two, it seems."

"And just who am I?"

"You," I said, "and I hate to mention this, since I'm sure you tolerate gross comments all the time, are the Doctor of Death, someone who deals in negative images. But that's all I've got figured out so far."

"Well, let me give you some material," he said then. I was right. "Will you come with me a minute? I have to make a phone call."

"Sure," I said. We strode through the bar area and past the phone inlaid in the mosaic surrounding what used to be a deco water fountain. Tom walked through the ceiling-high doors and into the last chamber I'd come through to get in. He walked up to the desk and nodded to the queen on duty. The queen pushed the phone to him.

"Thank you," he murmured. He dialed a number and leaned on the desk. He didn't look at me. "Hello, this is Doctor Sanders," he said after a minute. "Will you check the patient in 232, please?" He waited a moment. "Shit," he said then. "Thank you." He hung up. "Call back in five hours," he reported to me.

I could deal in his imagery. "Didn't the fucker die yet?" I asked.

He laughed arrantly. "No. Not yet."

"Shit," I said. Tom snickered again.

As we walked back into the Club I thought about what I was doing with this sick queen who reveled in his work as a pathologist and his hobby of observation. There was definitely nothing sexual in what was pulling us together; but something was attracting us and I was sure we both felt it. To some extent, it was a mutual fascination with observation but one that had no defined limits or polite boundaries: a twisted willingness to contention. There was something sick about this.

Old money from Uruguay

There were more people to meet that night. It was T time: THC time, well into Sleaze, the morning music, when everyone took THC and moonwalked. I walked happily down the marble stairs in the front of the Club, my hand sliding down the bannister. It was probably 11 a.m. but it was, after all, a party and there were a few hours left.

At the bottom of the stairs two Holy Spirit employees hurried past carrying a man in a straitjacket. I stood there and watched them rush him into the nurse's office as a black door I hadn't noticed before opened up, a woman's face appeared, and they were admitted. Then the door closed and the scene was over.

My hand was still on the bannister. I looked up as thirty or forty fan dancers came down the stairs and I made room for them. They smiled at me as they passed and I smiled back, figuring I was a representative of another type.

I spotted Tom Sanders in the living room, hanging out on one of the banquettes with a bare-chested man in eye makeup. He had on white pants, a sailor's cap and spike heels. About thirty, I figured, a dark skinned, cleanshaven man and his hair was thinning from what I could see under the cap.

I walked over and he was saying, "They hired me to stamp out bitches. Shit."

He was saying this and strutting around like he couldn't stop moving in his high heels. "Shit," he said, his dark Latin face dripping with derision and he made half his face hang down with the word. "They can't throw me out of here yet. I want to get my money's worth. I paid good money to get in here."

Tom went over to the bar to get us some juices. Santos turned to me. "So are you having a good time, baby?" he asked me quickly.

"Why, yeah, sure," I said.

"Your friend Tom is an absolute pleasure," he said. "A gentleman. What does he do for a living?"

"He's an M.D.," I said. "A pathologist."

"Ah," Santos glanced at his friend Julio and said something quickly in Spanish. "I beg your pardon," he apologized immediately. "For a moment I forgot we're not in La Fangito. The Bronx," he added.

"Oh."

"What do you do for a living?" he asked me.

"I'm a researcher in an advertising agency," I said.

He nodded. "So tell me, honey, you're working this nerd look, aren't you?"

"What do you mean?" I asked, figuring I'd better be somewhat assertive.

"You know what I mean, honey," he said kindly. "Grow up."

Tom came back then with four plastic cups balanced in his hands.

"Thank you, darling," Santos said, still through his dark glasses. He accepted the first glass. "Here, Julio," he said to the figure sitting in the darkness behind us.

28

Julio came forward to accept the drink. He was wearing an intricate body stocking, he had straight black hair and his deepset black eyes were heavily and darkly made up. "Thank you," he said huskily to Tom.

"You're welcome," Tom said with the proper amount of deference. I wanted to know about all this, but he refused to look at me until he handed me my drink.

"Santos was just kind enough to inquire about my evening," I told Tom.

"Oh, real-lee," Tom said.

"Yes, that's right," Santos said immediately and adjusted his sailor's cap to a slight tilt. He began to strut again. "We are keeping count," he declared and he put his drink down. "We are keeping count and we are keeping a scoreboard right there over the entrance to this Club, and we are going to add up the points and *then* we are going to give out awards." He looked me full in the face and I knew this was dead serious. I was wide eyed. Tom laughed.

"That's right," Santos said, still addressing me. He turned for a moment to look at Tom, laughing, then he dismissed him and turned back to me. "The rest of them are all adding up all these other numbers. They're walking around with their SAT scores and honey, I say, 'Please' to that. We are adding up other numbers here.

"We are going to give out Miss New Social Find de la Saison," he said. "We are going to give out Miss Most Really Most Fabulous," he went on, stopping and turning. Tom was applauding.

"We are going to give out Miss Most Prescient Sneakers," he said finally and his tambourine shivered.

"And to you," he said to Tom, "we won't even give an award because, darling, you know what's going on. And so does Harold. The two of you know what's going on here. Now Julio and I must go," he said abruptly. "We have to finish getting our money's worth." He smiled and Julio came forward slowly. They were off.

"It was nice meeting you," I called after him.

"Girl," Tom drawled.

"Who were they?" I asked him.

"I don't know," he laughed. "I just met them."

"Well, they seemed to know you," I said.

"Yes, they did, didn't they," Tom said. He put his cigarette to his mouth then took it away. "I have to tell you who you were fooling with there."

"So you do know them," I said.

"No, not exactly," he said. "Santos was at a party I went to last summer on Fire Island. We weren't actually introduced. I'm afraid I was so overstated as to compliment him on his tambourine. Afterwards someone came up to me and explained that while Santos was standing there on Fire Island, taking drugs and dancing at a pool house, people were starving in Uruguay. He and his family emigrated to the United States. They are old money from Uruguay."

"He said he was from the Bronx," I said.

Tom nodded. "Old money from Uruguay," he said.

Sunglasses at night

Later I was rushing through the bar area. Although I didn't have any direction or destination I was in a hurry. I heard someone call "Harold," and I stopped and turned around, clutching my cardigan. I looked around through my spectacles.

"Over here," I heard and I turned in the direction of one of the banquettes in the outer circle. There was a woman, I figured maybe about forty, in Wrangler jeans and a T-shirt and with a long pony tail. She had very white skin and large dark glasses. She was sitting there with an ethyl rag in her mouth.

I stepped closer and I saw long red nails on that white hand held delicately to the rag in her mouth. I leaned forward. "Did you call me?" I asked.

She kept staring at me with her rag in her mouth. She was looking into my eyes, but flatly. Then, slowly, she took the rag away and, like an automaton, she put it down beside her.

"Yes?" she said.

"I'm Harold," I said, holding out my hand. "You just called me."

"I did?" she asked. "Oh well. I'm Mary. How do you do?"

"Swell, thank you," I said.

"What are you, some kind of twinkie?" she asked me.

31

"I should say not," I said. "I'm twenty-seven."

"A twinkie," she said and turned her head away and then back. She sat into the banquette. "I don't think we've ever met before," she said. "Have you been coming here long?"

"No," I said. "I'm new here." I sat down next to her. "I think it's very interesting. But I don't tell people that."

"'Interesting,'" she said. "Yes, I agree it's 'interesting.' That's why I've been coming to this Club since it opened. Not to mention I like men. I'm horny," she said blankly.

"Oh?" I said.

"Yes," she went on. "I am. I always am. That's what I find 'interesting.' And here I can find what 'interests' me."

"Which is?" I felt I should ask.

"S&M," she said. "Heavy S&M."

"I see," I said, impressed; and she could see it. "Yes, I would imagine this would be a good hunting ground."

"It's alright," she said. "But it's certainly not the Mineshaft or even one of Norm's orgies. But of course in those environments you more or less have to sacrifice the drugs." She looked around at some of the guys passing in front of us. "Hi, Mary," one of them called. "Hi," she answered, sort of generically.

"Don't get me wrong," she returned to me. "Those guys do drugs. You have your poppers, your coke, even your MDA. But it's not like here. I come here to do my ethyl. You want a hit?" she asked me.

"Why yes, I'd love some," I said.

"Here." She handed me the bottle and the rag. I started to spray it and she took it away from me.

"Twinkies," she muttered. She bunched up the rag into one corner around her fist and doused it. She handed it to me soaked and I put it in my mouth. I held it there the way I'd seen her do.

I tripped for a few minutes. When it was over I handed back her rag. "Thanks." I stood up. "It was nice meeting you, Mary," I said. I didn't want to risk boring her.

"Bye." Either she receded or I took off. I was too high and I don't remember. Anyway, it was a lot of activity for me, even for the Opening Party.

Tom

"Harold, how fast do you type?" Tom asked me. This was on Tuesday of that next week, and it was in the middle of the night, or it might as well have been. I was completely burnt out from dancing on the weekend and I'd crashed at 8 p.m. Now it was midnight.

"Hold on," I said. I rolled over and felt around on the floor for my glasses. "Who is this?" I asked. I put them on and sort of leaned up with the phone in my hand.

"Tom Sanders," he said. "I had to call you, Harold. Now just how fast do you type? Robert DiBlaisi said you know how to type and I need emergency assistance."

"Did Robert also tell you I think you're insane? But what's going on? What do you need?"

"I have this paper I have to submit, like tomorrow morning to my chairman, and Harold, I do not exaggerate when I tell you that the entirety of my career depends on this. The entirety of my future."

"And you need me to come uptown and type this for you right now."

"Would you, Harold?" he asked me. "Would you get in a cab right now and come up here? I wouldn't ask if this wasn't an emergency and believe me, I know how to judge emergencies."

"OK, sure," I said. I wrote down the address in Washington Heights. "But wait a minute.

Robert DiBlaisi also told me that you never allow anyone up to your apartment."

"That's right," he said. "That's why I live so far uptown. It's far enough away so that no one will insist on visiting me, and it's still New York. So that should convince you," he concluded, "of the absolute severity of this situation."

"OK, give me an hour," I said, and in that time I was showered, dressed and in a cab somewhere around 137th Street.

The cab pulled up to the only highrise in the neighborhood, the only cut glass lobby in the ride among six story tenements and even abandoned buildings.

I rode the elevator up to the thirty-second floor. When I got out and found the apartment, Tom opened the door just as I was about to knock.

"Hah, Harold," he said. "Boy, am I glad you were able to make it." He was wearing his black running suit from the past weekend, but his feet were bare and he had a day's growth on his face. "Come on in," he said.

Silently and cautiously, I handed him my jacket. I walked past a palm tree, and walked steadily down the hall into his bedroom. A queen size bed, an unmade tangle of sheets I wouldn't have wanted to look too closely at, was placed in the center. Huge thick books, medical books, I guessed, were piled, some opened, in stacks around the floor. There was a six foot bird cage to the side, newspapers scattered around the floor around it, but no bird. And covering the wall behind the bed, copper lame ran its length and width. It was draped, carefully arranged, though it'd started to fall on one side.

Tom stood behind me as I looked around, mesmerized. "Don't mind the mess," he kicked some shoes away. "I've been doing laundry all day and the rest of the apartment's a mess. That's why this proposal isn't finished yet, because I had to take two whole hits of acid to get all that laundry done."

"Tom," I said, turning to look at him. "You didn't really do two whole hits, did you?"

"Course I did," he said pointedly. "I had to get that laundry done. Now don't you tell anyone this, Harold Fenestere, but I hadn't done laundry in three, say four, months. I was getting to have a problem here."

"Didn't you run out of anything?"

"No," he said. "That's why there was so much laundry, because I have so many clothes. I must have at least a hundred and fifty pair of underwear."

"Stop," I said, holding up my hand. "And I promise not to even try to calculate if that's enough underwear to last every day for four months."

The errant bird made its appearance at that moment, hanging on to the doorjamb leading into the bathroom by its feet. It spread its wings and let out a loud screech.

"The flora," Tom explained, "and the fauna." A toothpick bobbed between his teeth.

"Tom," I said, "that bird is huge. That wingspan must be four feet."

"Oh, at least," he said and the bird screeched at me again. "Baby says Hello," he explained.

"Listen," I said. "You can freak me out or we can turn our energy to something practical and I can type your paper. Where's your typewriter?"

"In my other room," he said. "That's another reason I live uptown, so I could afford a two room apartment."

The other room was piled with cartons, there was a table in the middle, and a sofa. The sofa was covered with the four months' laundry. "Now here," Tom explained, pulling out a chair for me at the table in front of the typewriter.

I sat down and immediately covered my eyes. "Oh, Tom," I said. "Please do something about that. I cannot look at those specimens while I'm typing. I couldn't look at them while I was doing anything."

"Gosh, Harold," he said. "I'm sorry. I didn't know you were squeamish."

"I don't think I'm squeamish," I said looking again at the array of jars of viscous liquids and floating organs. "I'm just getting sick to my stomach at the sight of viscera. Please take them away."

"OK," he said, covering the jars with some of the laundry. "So long as you're not squeamish." I cleared a space next to the typewriter and looked at his copy.

"Wait," he said. He put on his white M.D. jacket. "For the effect," he said. "Effect is everything."

I sat down and looked at the papers again. "OK, just give me a few minutes to see if I understand what you want," I said. I read through the copy. "OK," I said. "I think I'm set," and started to type. Tom sat down diagonally across the table from me. I looked up from the Selectric over my glasses and he was watching me.

"Are you going to just hang over me while I type?" I asked.

"Sorry, Harold," he said. He lit a cigarette and looked away while his bare feet tapped the floor. I kept typing. Words like "initial studies" and several interdisciplinary hyphenations in quotations gave me the idea that Tom was working on something that was a new sub-field. As I typed further, I understood that he was requesting permission to direct his residency into a hybrid of two pathological roads of inquiry.

He smoked while I typed. Finally I finished. "Thank God that's over with," he said, sitting there in his white jacket, examining the final page.

"Thank God," I agreed.

"Whew, I am so exhausted," he said. "I have not slept since two nights ago."

"You're kidding," I said.

"No, I wouldn't kid about that. I am exhausted but it'll be at least another twelve to fourteen hours before I can sleep again. I am so wound up.

"Plus," he went on, "I spoke with my mother tonight. My mother's a doctor too and she's the one who convinced me I had to get this proposal in tomorrow after we talked over the structure of my request, and the internal politics. That's why I had to call you at the last minute."

"Your mother's a doctor, too?" I asked. "Robert said it was your father."

"Oh, both my parents are doctors," he said. "And both of my grandparents on my mother's side."

"You're kidding," I said. "What ethnic background are you?" I asked.

"I'm a wasp," he said. "Why?"

"Well, only because it's unusual in my experience, as a third generation immigrant ethnic,

38

for any of my friends to have that kind of educational family history. Everybody I know is like, the first college graduates in their families. How come you didn't ask your father for his advice, too?" I asked. "Is he in a different field or something?"

"Well, he is," Tom explained. "But my parents are divorced so it's not like he was there anyway when I happened to call my mother for her professional opinion."

"Wow," I said. "That's unusual for me, too. No one I know has parents who are divorced."

"Oh, it's quite common among wasps," Tom said. He sat back. Evidently he was relaxing a little.

"So you come from a line of women who know how to deal with men," I said.

"Except for myself of course." He sat back with his bare feet up on the chair smoking as he talked to me. "I spent the entirety of my adolescence in love with a boy who became my best friend, essentially because I worked on him and almost made him become my friend. We were best friends all throughout high school and during the whole time I went to college, right up until the time I left for New York."

"Did you ever sleep with him?"

"We slept in the same bed plenty of times, but that's all. I was so in love with him I didn't want to ruin anything. And I'm sure he loved me too. When he found out that I smoked pot, he asked me if I ever did and I admitted it, I said yes. And he cried."

"Wow," I said. "You were in love with him all that time. That must have been ten years. That's better than my story of teenage love. I was only in love with a boy in my high school class for three years. He did me the big favor of graduating early so I at least had senior year in peace. He was the first and last Italian-American I was ever in love with."

"Italian-Americans are fabulous, aren't they," Tom speculated. "That's why I came to New York. For people like Robert DiBlaisi."

I didn't want to hear that whole topic again. "I have to get going," I said. "It must be five a.m. and I have to get downtown and start getting ready for work."

"OK," he said, standing up. "I'll drive you. And here," he said as we stepped into the hallway. "This is for you. This palm tree is a present for you, Harold. I want you to have it. Come on, I'll carry it downstairs."

He picked up the King palm, already grown four feet high. It must have weighed fifty pounds. He hugged it to him as I opened the door for us and rang for the elevator. When we got downstairs daylight was coming up.

"How are we going to get through this day?" Tom said, looking around.

I held out two capsules of crystal in my hand. "Girl," Tom said, "you came prepared, didn't you?" We popped them into our mouths and swallowed them dry. I salivated a few times to help it down.

"I'll go get my car from the garage," Tom said. "You wait here with the palm tree." He went back into the building as I stood at the curb with the tree. Daylight was coming up stronger now. I put on my sunglasses and waited for Tom.

Butch lessons

When I went to the gym the sign over the reception desk said, "Girl, Don't Even Try It." In smaller type it added, "Bathing Suits Now Required in Wet Area." The glass door was taped with a five foot X.

"Hello, Mrs. Rizello," I said to Anthony, the cleanshaven crewcut receptionist. He was tall and very muscular. "Bobby walked through it," he explained about the glass door. "You know how she is, she just runs right through everywhere."

"She's worse in the disco," I said.

"Oh, I *know,*" Anthony said.

"The worst is when the speed makes her eyes bug out," I said.

"You mean like this?" he asked, opening his eyes as wide as he could. Bobby showed up on the other side of the reception area. He waved and pointed to his office.

I followed him across the gym floor. "What's up?" I asked.

Bobby shut the door. "I just wanted to give you a chance to read me in private," he said.

"You've lost your mind," I said. "Or I missed something, so it doesn't matter. May I take a raincheck?"

"'Can,'" Bobby corrected. "Don't ever say 'may.' Use basic words whenever you can."

"You mean like 'maybe' instead of 'perhaps?'"

"Right," Bobby said. "And try to throw in a couple of butch things, like how you just rode your bike there, or how you can't cook."

"I really can't cook," I said.

"See," the director of the gym said. "You're butch to begin with."

"That's a relief," I said. "I've been trying."

I yawned, then apologized. "I'm sorry," I said. "I was up all last night with Tom Sanders."

"Tom Sanders?" Bobby said. He ran his hand over his crewcut and looked around, his eyes bulging. "That crazy thing? Did you know, he hasn't had sex in two years?"

"I don't believe that story. Anyway, tell me more about your date last night."

"He's really nice," Bobby said. "I'm seeing him tonight for the fourth night in a row."

"How old is he?" I asked.

"He'll be twenty-five soon," Bobby said. I laughed. "I don't know why," Bobby said, "but there's something about him being twenty-four that seems young."

"But you're only twenty-six," I said.

"But everyone thinks I'm thirty."

"Thirty-two was what that kid you picked up at Uncle Charlie's said."

"Shutup," Bobby said. "Anyway, he's twenty-four and he's really nice."

"Why is he so nice?" I asked. "He's not another Est graduate, is he?"

"No, he's the one who made a face when I mentioned Est. Thank God."

"Thank God," I agreed.

"All that Est shit, that Lakewood stuff, it's all about Making It Happen. They tell you 'Make it happen, Make it happen,' and then if you really want to make it happen, take the advanced course."

"So this is your fourth date in four nights?" I asked.

"Yeah. But I don't care about that counting shit."

"I agree," I said. "Those numbers and rules and things certainly don't matter by now."

"So we went on this first date," Bobby said. "I went over to his house and he had all these things circled in the *Village Voice.* So I picked one. I should have known better by the address, it was something like 539 East 13th Street, way down by Avenue C. We climbed up these stairs and into this room and they stamp your hand. There were these hippies, I swear to God, Harold, there were these like, post-hippies, these beatniks banging drums saying, 'This is my work, this is my work.'"

"You're not serious," I said.

"I am," Bobby answered. "And with slides. On a sheet. I looked around me and I figured at five dollars a head this is some racket for people who don't want to work. And we couldn't leave, there was no intermission. Then I looked down at the stamp on my hand and I saw the word 'Wage.' It said, 'End wage slavery.' That's when I looked at him and we got up and left."

The Queen of S&M

Mary sat back in the banquette. It was late in the morning. "God, how I miss the good old days...."

"You mean the first couple of years here?" I asked.

"Yes," she said. "Those were the good old days. Back then there were No Women. There were me and maybe two or three others: Susan, Celeste, Joannie, the tall Japanese-American lesbian with long hair. And her ex-lover, who's since disappeared. She used to wear a mohawk and every week she'd dye it a different color."

"That tall woman is Joannie?" I asked. "Who's the shorter one, this really stylish Japanese woman who looks like she's a model or a designer or something?"

"I don't know her," Mary said.

"She dances at eleven o'clock," I said. "And I never see her down here in the bar area. What's her name?"

"I don't know," Mary said again. "I'll find out." I'd made a mistake. Mary didn't like not knowing things. "But there were five women, tops," she rushed on. "And there weren't any twinkies."

"Well, then how did all the thirty-five-year-olds get to be thirty-five?" I asked. "They must have been in their twenties some time."

"All I know," she said mordaciously, "is that it used to be different here. It used to be all men in

44

full leathers. It used to be men. You were lucky if you could walk through the balcony it was so packed with men having sex. Oh, how I miss that. If you think it's crowded now on a Saturday night, you should've seen it then. The kind of crowd you get here now for a party used to be the regular Saturday night. The lines were a block long in both directions, six thousand people attending, 99.9% of whom were men. It was always six deep at the bar. Now it's only three and four deep."

She shifted her position. "And if you wanted to bring a woman, you had to phone weeks in advance. There was a list. And if your woman guest acted out, you got a letter. It wasn't uncommon for a female guest to be told she was too femme. All that's changed. Thank God they still don't allow dresses or high heels. And when you got a letter, the envelope didn't even have the Club name on it, that's how private it was. You felt protective of the Club; it was private, a secret you didn't tell. You never mentioned the Club's name to anyone."

"But I don't," I said. "I wouldn't even think of saying it to anyone."

"I'm glad to hear that, but it's not good enough. There used to be movies shown in the dome on Sunday nights. Did you know that above the balcony is the old projection room?"

"No," I said. "I've never been up to the balcony. I think there's still some sex going on up there."

"And that's another thing that's changed." She turned to face me but I couldn't see her eyes behind her glasses. It seemed she wasn't really looking at me. "Did you know there used to be free beer here all night, not just until four a.m.?

Now I hear they're going to get rid of the nurse next season. How about the night in the first season there was a blizzard and only forty people showed up? Not that the rest didn't try. Warren played the weather report as the ball came down. But all that's over. Now you don't even see any of the guys who used to come here then."

"Well, what happened to them?" I asked. "If they just left, then they gave up on the Club."

"Calm down," she said. "Would you like a hit of ethyl?"

"Well, alright," I said, and she produced two rags. We each did a hit.

"So tell me more," I said.

"Did you know this Club is 40,000 square feet built in three levels?" she asked me.

I shook my head, fascinated.

"And the dance floor is an oval; it's not per-fectly round. The dome sits over it, constructed over the balcony and beneath the old projection room." Her hands twitched as she spoke, and her red fingernails were two inches long. She bowed her head, her face was perfectly white, and her brown hair hung down the back in a pony tail. She looked like a penitent, rather than a serious club denizen.

"How do you know all this?" I asked.

"Because I've read the floor plans. I have a copy of them at home. Somewhere. And because I've lived in this neighborhood all my life. My grandfather lived on St. Mark's Place, and I grew up on Avenue A before moving to Stuyvesan-town."

"You live in Stuytown?" I asked.

"Sure," she said cooly, lighting a cigarette. I couldn't reconcile the image of this S&M domi-

natrix and ethyl mistress, this nightlife professional, living such a middle class real life. She let
everything she was aware of, everything she was
involved in there, confront basic realities. She
probably wore a cloth coat. I thought that was
fabulous.

"Well," I said, looking around, "I guess your
men are starting to arrive."

"You're right," she said lubriciously. "I hope
Evan's here," she added and playfully touched
her tongue to her lips. Now I couldn't believe she
was being coquettish.

I also knew I was supposed to ask. "Who's
Evan, one of your slaves?"

"Oops," she said. "You know him, he dances
at six o'clock. Always wears shorts, has a beard.
Insists he's a top. But I'm going to find out."

"What are you going to do?" I asked.

"Well, for starters, I guess I'm going to have to
get rid of his lover, Miguel. I mean just get him
out of the way, temporarily. I don't want to interfere with their relationship." Not much she
didn't, but it was nothing to me. "I don't suppose
you'd be interested in taking a former Mr. Leather first runner-up off my hands, would you?"

"What would I have to do?" I asked.

"Nevermind," she said. "If you have to ask,
nevermind. Here comes someone who looks
more like your type," she added. Robert came up
to me.

"Mary, this is Robert," I made the introductions. Introductions were a very big part of Club
life there. You couldn't speak to someone unless
you'd been formally introduced.

"I've seen you around," Mary said. "You're
very all-American."

Robert cleared his throat. "I've seen you around, too," he said. "You're not."

"You're right," she said, pleased. "Well, I'd better get on with my man-hunt," she said for Robert's benefit.

"It was nice meeting you," he said, completing the requisite formalities.

"See you later." She got up and walked away.

"Her who?" he turned to me.

"You heard her," I said.

"It figures you'd be friends with Ethyl Mary," he said. "Here, hold this," he said and I held his drink for him while he lit a cigarette, something we'd been through before a thousand times in a hundred clubs. He stood there holding his cigarette and screwed up his face while he thought about it. He took back his drink and leaned against the banquette while he watched the passing guys.

"Now tell me that isn't my type," he nodded at one of them.

"Now you sound like Mary," I said.

"Is that what you two talk about?" he asked, his eyes getting larger.

"No," I said. "She tells me about people she ties up and also some disco history."

"People she ties up," he repeated.

"Robert," I said, "I've known you too long for you to start acting demure now."

"Acting what?" he said, falling back on his background.

"I mean I can remember a story or two about a trip to the Mineshaft."

"And you were with me the entire time and all we did was walk through it."

"But that was your second visit there," I said.

"I had to check it out first to see if you could handle it. You couldn't. Like evidently you can't handle here."

"What does that mean?"

"Ethyl Mary," he repeated. "I bring him to this Club and who does he become friends with but Tom Sanders and Ethyl Mary."

"I thought you'd be proud of me," I said.

"You know what I heard about her? I heard she's the Queen of S&M. I heard the only time she was ever speechless was when some guy said to her he wanted to cut off her head and fuck the stump. And you're friends with her."

"Not yet," I said. "But I'm going to be." I watched her walking up the black iron stairs to the dance floor. She stopped to talk to some other deferential audience.

I respected her, and Santos, and all the other people I saw there. These people made a career of style and fun and they had the highest standards for both. I thought this was an accomplishment.

"And please," Robert said. "I heard all those things Tom said about me, about my being the perfect Italian-American. He should only know I'm part Jewish."

"Well, I don't think Tom really understands the melting pot concept to that extent. Anyway, as long as he doesn't start classifying me with the other Italian-Americans, I don't care."

"No. He's probably got you in some group by yourself. Where you belong. And I do really think he might be crazy. Did you hear that story about the boy he was in love with all those years? He must love to torture himself. Anyway, I just want it made perfectly clear," Robert said. He cleared his throat. "That whatever trip you and Tom Sanders are going on, I have no intention of making it with you. I'm not watching The Adventures of Tom Sanders and Harold Fenestere."

I blinked. "Why?"

"Because I can see you getting carried away. All that talk about something going on on the dance floor. If you're going to have some kind of experience, you have to understand that not everyone else is approaching it the same way."

"So you're saying that you don't know what I'm talking about."

"I'm saying," Robert said, "that I don't want to talk about it at all."

"OK," I said. Later on, other people couldn't understand how Robert and I didn't spend a lot of time together at The Holy Spirit, but people who are friends a long time can make these kinds of adjustments when they're needed.

I was more than willing to admit I'd turned The Holy Spirit into a religion; or at least I was in the process of doing that. I made the d.j. the high priest; the women members represented goddess worship; the disco ball in the ceiling was a fertility ritual. And more, I was trying to figure out what happened with the energy created on the dance floor. It was created, it rose, and it was contained explosively under the dome. There was more to this, but I still hadn't figured it out.

But there was one mistake I made in my premises then: I thought everyone else had made it a religion too and they were just being fabulous in not talking about it. But it turned out later I was wrong about that.

Ablutions

The Club became a weekly habit. October gave way to November and as I learned the season's calendar, I began to see how the Club had taken gay events and made traditions of them: especially the White Party and the Black Party. Parties were religious observances and served the same function. Management took mainstream holidays and created our own calendar of movable feasts: their Thanksgiving was our Night People Party and their Easter would be our Land of Make Believe. I was shocked when the Christmas Party was called the Christmas Party.

The Dance Club became the thing we lived for as the real question of what we were living for was happily suborned. We looked forward to our Club every Saturday and spent the week preparing for it, shopping for clothes to dance in, working out and getting our hair cut. Are you going out this weekend, we'd ask girlfriends we knew less well than others. Darling, of course I'm going, they'd say.

On Saturdays you fasted so your drugs'd work better that night. Drugs were budgeted somewhere after rent and before utilities. And then after the event itself we spent Monday and Tuesday crashing as the new week started and the cycle began again. I wore sunglasses to work and didn't take them off until Wednesday and if

I couldn't handle what I saw, they were back on by Thursday. And since the drugs we took required a week to pass through our systems and we took more before that ever happened, I don't think we came down that entire year.

I was meeting Bobby after he got off from the gym, on Christopher Street. Coming from the East Village I took a long route, past Great Jones Street. I meandered around Lafayette Street, around Houston. The old manufacturing buildings there were now loft spaces though most of them were still under renovation or still under negotiation and rockers lived in some of them. I passed this old steel diner on Houston. Lean, long haired guys in black jeans and converse sneakers, hidden in sunglasses, sat on the ground with girls with spiked hair, pleated skirts and leather jackets. Johnny Sex stood there shirtless, pale, his chest all corded muscles. His python draped around his neck reaching the hips of his jeans.

Approaching Cooper Union and Astor Place I saw the evening turning grey, the air kind of purple and dark blue early fall, a time when it always looked like it was about to do something, maybe rain. The tenements looked foreboding and interesting, like the most fascinating, disenfranchised people probably live there. I wondered again about the Japanese woman from the dance floor, but I couldn't picture her living anywhere. She seemed so absolutely indigenous to the dance floor, I thought she must only exist there, summoned up, from Saturday to Saturday. But what I really wanted to know was, did she know who I was or was it all in my head? Maybe nobody there knew anybody else and I was imagining the whole thing; I always felt I was being watched there but maybe I was imagining that, too. And Robert had said I was overreading.

I cut over to East Ninth Street and then crossed Sixth Avenue as Ninth disappeared into Christopher. People were hurrying home from work. I thought about my job. It just seemed so contrived compared to what I saw people doing in The Holy Spirit.

A familiar looking blond, short, well built and goodlooking, passed by and those credentials alone indicated he was someone from the circuit. I recognized him, though, and I could identify him by his dance step (he looked like he was boxing), what he wore to dance (a tight black one piece), where he danced (nine o'clock), and who he danced with (someone not as goodlooking as he was). But this was the secret information about someone, I thought as I met up with Bobby and Richard.

"Look at that guy," Bobby said.

"She's absolutely beautiful," Richard said in perfect English that made me remember what one queen called him, the Queen of Caracas.

"I think she's looking at us," Bobby said, and I remembered what the same queen had called Bobby, a Long Island Jewish Debutante.

"I think she's looking at *me*," Richard said.

"You're crazy," Bobby said. "Here, let's see." Bobby walked away from us and stood on the other side of the blond kid, prominent in the crowd on West Street. It created a frieze, this disparate group in front of the bar. The blond kid seemed to be separated from the people he was with, a moat of space around him. Off to the right was Bobby, observing and appraising calmly,

53

and to the left, Richard, leering, and me. I was disinterested.

Richard, the Queen of Caracas, walked all around in an oblique circle that encompassed the characters, making contortions with his face and sounding invocations. It either looked like da Vinci or Hieronymus Bosch. He was really making jokes about the situation and reading Bobby. Bobby didn't move. The kid's eyes stayed on his friends, but they were large and aware, indicating he knew he was the center of their attention and the center of the larger circle too.

Richard completed his circle and I went to join him. "Bobby is so bizarre," he pronounced. "He actually thinks that kid is looking at him."

"Is he?" I asked.

"I don't know, he might be," Richard said.

Bobby came back and joined us. "Let's do something else," Bobby said. "I'm tired of cruising. Let's have dinner."

"We could ask Brian Owen to join us," Richard said. "I saw him earlier in Ty's."

"Not Brian Owen," Bobby said. "He's been behaving like he has a problem lately."

"Who cares?" I said. "This is fun. I love hanging out here. I just completely love it."

"So do I," Richard said emphatically.

"I'll be right back," Bobby said, and disappeared back around the corner we'd just turned. "I'll meet you at the restaurant," he called.

Richard turned to me. "Are you going this weekend?" he asked.

"Of course I am," I said. "Who's spinning?"

There was a pause. "Shaun," Richard answered finally, as neutrally as he could. "It's the Black Party."

"I just moved," I explained. "I haven't gotten all my mail yet."

"Oh, I know how that is," Richard said graciously as we walked through the crowd. Bobby was talking with Brian Owen. "I'm glad you're here," Richard said. He looked at Brian unflinchingly. "Bobby said you act like you have some sort of problem."

Inside ethyl chloride

At the Black Party last year someone got fisted on stage and then they shaved his head. The year before there was a circumcision. I'm glad I wasn't there even if that makes me a big woman or something.

This year's invitation said the Black Party would be an art installation. When I ran into Mary she naturally complained that the whole plan lacked balls. "Last year," she said, recalling one of her famous last years. "Last year I carried a bull whip. I don't know how I did it," she began modestly. "But I snapped it across the locker room and it flicked some poor guy's cigarette right out of his mouth. The locker room security patrol couldn't believe it. This year you'd be lucky to see a bull whip, let alone see one in action. I'm certainly not going," she added in a staccato.

"Yeah," I said. "I gathered."

When I stepped into the living room at this year's Black Party I was confronted with massive silk screens, huge canvasses propped at the highest levels above different banquettes. They were billboard-sized renderings of undressed men. I walked upstairs to the dance floor and I saw Mary, so I climbed up on the banquette next to her to say hello.

"Come here," she said and motioned upward. I climbed up farther and we were at the top level of the banquettes. The music was pounding loudly across the dome, the lights vibrating across our faces. She silently handed me her ethyl bottle and her rag so I sprayed some on and stuffed it in my mouth, sitting back against the arced wall of the dome.

Then I lost a dimension, visually. I felt like I was directly above the dance floor but from far away with star light projecting around me. I felt like a star at that moment, like a nova energy unit, equal to every other, and this was empowering.

I looked at Mary. "This is your Club," she nodded.

"Thank you for showing me that," I said.

"Good luck, kid," she said.

I jumped down to join the dancers, my people, I actually thought, expansively. My feet hit ground and my body moved into the dance floor. I looked around while I was travelling. All the familiar dancers were performing their routines; tonight all in black. As far as I could see across the dance floor, there were moving and travelling black figures cohering into that *larger thing*. The blue and purple haze moving across the dance floor rose and shifted with the dancers.

I danced past twelve o'clock and peered down the black portal entrance. There was the proscenium, from when this was a concert hall. A stage, like this was theater when it couldn't get any more real than this. Fabulous irony, I thought.

I looked up again at the haze travelling over our heads. Real life only existed there, Saturdays. I couldn't believe it was only a week since I'd been there.

Tom Sanders danced by. I looked out of the corner of my eye and suddenly became aware of myself dancing. I decelerated abruptly and I separated from the movement. Tom looked at me and said, "Hello, Harold. What are you doing, dancing?"

I was shocked that he caught me in a moment of self-awareness, at the exact moment that I was thinking about dancing instead of actually dancing. Obviously I hadn't underestimated him at all. "Hello, Tom," I said. "That was very perspicacious of you."

He started to clap. "That's fabulous," he said.

"What are you talking about?" I said.

"Robert tells me you have all sorts of theories about this discotheque," he said. "Tell me some of them."

"Tom," I said, "you are talking on the dance floor."

"Please, Harold," he said. "Just tell me one. I'll show you my rhinestones. Look," he said. He turned sideways, displaying his upper arm. An ornate deco rhinestone was strapped around his tricep.

"Tom," I intoned, "that's beautiful."

"Isn't it?" he asked in a low voice. "Now, look at this," he said harshly, and quickly turned around and flexed his bare pectoral. A hologram was fixed to it. He pulsed his muscle again and the image on his chest changed.

"Now I've shown you one of the other things I came to New York for," he said. "To wear rhinestones, to act out in any way I please. Now tell me one of your theories."

"Well," I said, thinking of the night I did a hit of ethyl and looked up and something above me laughed. "One of the first things I learned here, one of the first things the place taught me," I corrected myself, "is that everything's the same as everything else. Ultimately there's no need for reconciliation or resolution."

"That's fabulous," he said hoarsely and I knew I was in trouble.

"If you take an oblique enough view," I said. "We're probably all something like grey bulbous cells tangential to each other. We're separate grey cells to the extent we're individuals in this lifeform but, as you step back, you see these grey round balls in clusters. Everything is a part of each other. Or, as The Holy Spirit said to me the first night, It's all the same anyway."

"Entropy," he said. "You've just defined entropy."

The light man, working in the control booth next to the d.j., put on a special projection: images of pills circulated the ceiling of the dome, generated through the star machine on top of the tree. Some of the crowd cheered; some people applauded the pictures of desoxyn, tuinal, valium and didrex. A beautiful cleanshaven Cuban boy with long hair danced past us. He stopped and kissed me hello as he passed. Tom just watched hesitantly.

"And what do you call that?" he asked me.

"Trite," I said. "Carlos is happy, and look at him dance, every movement a perfect expression of his inner lifeform and the personality of his spirit." Carlos danced by with his arm extended, shaking his finger. "I just love things that are trite," I said.

"And that is very trite," Tom nodded in Carlos' direction.

"Harold," John Jr. called and came up to me and put his arms around my neck. He was wearing a propeller cap and knickers and he claimed to be eighteen but people theorized he was about twelve.

"Not now, John," I said. "Uncle Thomas and I are talking."

His angular thin face contorted with jealousy. "You never let *me* talk to you on the dance floor," he said, churning his jaw.

"Go on," I said. "And let the grown ups talk."

"There's Himiko," John said. I watched him dance in and join the woman I'd been wondering about, who'd winked at me at the Opening Party. Himiko smiled at John and they started dancing together. Now I was sorry I'd sent him away.

Tom was watching all this. "I didn't know you knew Pee-Wee," he said.

"His name's John," I said.

"Oh, excuse me," Tom said. "I didn't know. Is he part of another theory of yours?"

"No," I said. "Just a game." I danced over behind John and put my arms over his shoulders. "Scenes from the Bible," I said to Tom. "We can play Abraham and Isaac." I turned from John and let him go back to his dancing. He was dancing with Celeste now.

"Scenes from the Bible," Tom said. "I love it."

"Don't you?" I asked. "And what better place than here?"

"That's right," he applauded and all of a sudden I became afraid that Himiko would see us talking so much on the dance floor. I walked off and wandered down the stairs. Tom followed me. On the video over the bar whole blocks of buildings were crashing, dynamited.

"And there's something else," I said turning to face Tom. Distractedly I looked at the ends of my

T-shirt. It wasn't torn or anything, but it was only half tucked in. "You remember the night we were introduced? I asked you about the feeling on the dance floor that was leading up to something."

"Come on, girl," he said.

"Haven't you given any further thought to that?" I asked him. "Someone should and I have. I'm sure you have too and that's partly why I don't trust you, Tom." He was clapping his hands. "Here's what I think is going on: The most creative people in New York, which could be the highest energy city on the planet, assemble here and take all this speed, right? Maybe the most energy this planet has ever seen is being generated here," I went on. Tom sat down on a banquette facing me. "Now think about the fact that the unique thing about this time in history is that Basic Conflict is manifested as large as it can grow. It's the U.S. and the U.S.S.R., and this Basic Conflict could blow up the planet. That's never been possible before. Tom," I said quickly and intently, "the planet could blow up right from here. When it happens it's going to happen right here when the high energy music reaches its highest point. That's why the sleaze music has that relief quality."

"I don't know," he said finally. "Anyway," he changed the subject. He looked at me, smirking. "I hear you're becoming friends with Ethyl Mary."

"Frankly," I said, "I'm a little frightened of her."

He grinned. "She's standing right behind you," he said in a low voice.

I turned around, terrified. There was no one there and Tom laughed. "You really are scared of her, aren't you?"

"Yes, I am," I said. "And if you had any sense, you'd be too."

"Aw, Mary's full of shit," he said.

"Shutup," I said. "Why are you looking for trouble when everything's going fine?"

"I don't know," he said, sitting down on a banquette facing the video. A scene from Querelle was on. "It's just my nature," he said cryptically. "To delve for pathology. What are you so nervous for?"

"I'm not nervous," I said. "My heart's just pumping and the adrenaline is flowing through my body."

"But you're not nervous," he said.

"No." I looked up at the back bar. A naked master was whipping his slave. Then I looked back at the video.

"What is this?" Tom asked me.

"Querelle," I said, straightening my glasses. "It's based on a story by Jean Genet. He spent most of his life in prisons and he had this association of fucking and death. See this scene where the big sailor brutalizes Querelle?"

"I like that," Tom said. He lit a cigarette and sat there, watching.

"Now watch this," I said. "See Querelle walking down this alley among the phallic shaped buildings? Now watch, see how this other guy walking this sexual path gets his throat slit. Genet considered brutal death and one man fucking another man synonymous. He saw it as the only way to take on another man's masculinity."

"I can follow that," Tom said. "Well, my God," he looked at his watch. "I almost forgot. I have to leave. Someone died last night and I have to perform the autopsy. Good night, Harold," he added. He kissed me and took off.

I stood there watching his twisting, retreating form beating a fast pace to the locker room. His head turned around and looked at me watching him and I thought of a gargoyle with its tongue distended. Maybe it was because it was the Black Party, but the gothic imagery seemed perfectly in place.

I encounter
the Diana People:
the cult of the woman

The next weekend I remember standing under a three-foot-high cocaine sculpture and a five-foot razor blade balanced over the back bar. A man in harem pants stood there twisting a tangerine scarf, entertaining his friends on a banquette. Then one of them jumped down next to him and started dancing back and forth with his own scarf.

I looked up and saw a young boy who was sitting on the top level of a banquette blowing soap bubbles. His haircut was Jersey City, longer on top, but trimmed in close furrows on the sides. Then a pride of pretty boys trolloped past, wearing oversized clothes on their thin frames, and two with straight hair had arranged it so that it that hung alluringly over their foreheads. One boy had black hair and another had blond; he wore a London Boy T-shirt. Another's was Eraserhead high and bleached. He wore black cotton sweat pants over black leather sneakers.

A young woman was at the front, talking attentively with the chosen escort of the moment. Her thick brown hair was pulled back Princess Leia style. As they passed, she excused herself from her partner, and came over to Tom and me. The boys stopped after a few paces, safely ahead of us where they could diplomatically avoid any acknowledgement which she, as a woman, could make without implication.

"Why Tom Sanders," she said somewhat nasally, leaning forward and kissing him on the cheek. "How are you?"

"Diana," he said reverently, returning the kiss. "Diana, I'd like you to meet my friend, Harold."

"How do you do," she asked me, offering her hand.

"It's a pleasure meeting you," I said, holding her hand with both of mine. I was entranced. She was warm and charming. I love women but I'd never met someone as appealing as Diana was.

"Would either of you boys know where I can get some acid?" she asked. "Test tube. I'm such a girl of the 90s."

I looked at Tom. "And the point is," I said, "you'd really have to be a girl of the 90s to even know you were."

"That's right," Tom said. He rubbed his nose. He was looking through a small plastic bag for a piece of acid. He held a minute paper under one of the light beams and then handed it to Diana.

"Here you go, girlfriend," he said. "And if you have any more visions of the 90s be sure to tell Harold or me."

"It was nice meeting you, Harold," she said. She rejoined her group; they proceeded up the stairs, thick in conversation with a correctly timed burst of small chatter and laughter.

Except for one older boy who was still standing there. "I'm David Walken," he said.

"You sure are, girl," Tom said.

"I'm Harold," I said.

"Yeah," Tom said. "David, Harold. I for one have no desire to see how this turns out," he said. "Excuse me," he added.

David stood there. His hair was curly and short and he came up to my shoulder. "But you did know who I was already, didn't you," he asked me through his glasses.

"Um, yeah, sure," I said through my glasses. "I saw you. But I thought you were one of the Stupid People." I put my hand over my mouth.

David's eyes widened and his mouth opened in delighted horror. "I didn't mean to say that out loud," I said. "I didn't mean that I thought anyone was like explicitly stupid. I just got the impression of your group that it was like, primarily visually intensive."

"That's OK," David said diplomatically. "I mean, there's definitely a case to be made either way." We sat down on a banquette. "Would you like some THC?" he asked.

"Is it T time yet?" I said. "I don't have a watch." I looked around for one.

From upstairs the music broke and everyone screamed and applauded. "Come on," David said. He walked ahead, stopped and then looked at me and waited while I joined him. We hurried up the black iron stairs in the back of the Club. At the twelve o'clock entrance we cautiously joined the crowd that was standing around the packed dome. The beginning choruses of "Eye In The Sky" circled around the room as the screaming started again. I stood next to David Walken. We both looked upwards as the trap door ceremoniously opened in the ceiling of the dome and the ball descended. "I am the eye in the sky," the

66

song rose. "I can read your mind," and the beats per minute accelerated. We applauded as the ball finished its descent into position above the tree.

"Come on," David said. "I mean, it's still T time."

We walked down to the landing behind the dance floor and sat on a carpeted banquette. David spooned out some T and I did it, then he did it. We watched the dance floor. From where we were sitting below twelve o'clock, the entrance looked like a movie screen. Things started to get a little opaque.

I looked at David out of the sides of my eyes. He looked at me the same way, dead serious and wide awake. We sat there attentively, rigid with speed.

"Do you ever feel like you're going to have a nervous breakdown here?" I asked him.

"Do you?" he said.

"Well, yeah." My heart was thumping madly. I was in a place where I could either be all alone and isolated among strangers, or I could resolve to feel secure. The THC was doing its act and I thought I was going to completely dissociate emotionally. "Yeah," I said again. "There are times when I feel like I could have a nervous breakdown right here. That I could just let go of my sanity. Then the only thing that keeps me from doing it is knowing that if I do, I won't be accomplishing anything because I'll still be there with myself. I'd be aware of the whole thing. All I'd do is lose my mind and embarrass myself publicly. It would be like being publicly incontinent."

"Do you hear the yadayada?" David asked.

"Of course I do," I said. My nerves were tingling from the MDA. I had to move so I stood up and started dancing.

"I just wish it would shutup sometime," David went on. "Sometimes I really can't *bear* listening to that voice. It just goes on and on. And on."

"And on," I said. "I just wish we didn't have to think about anything. I mean, that's why we take drugs, isn't it? God, people think going to the disco is easy." I was still dancing while I was speaking. "I mean, we come here to address the meaninglessness of life. They have no idea how hard this is. Or what's involved," I concluded.

"No idea," David said, getting up and dancing next to me. He moved around in a circle, leaning over and clapping his hands.

"I mean," I said dancing, "this is work. Does anyone think it's easy, trying not to obsess on an idea when you're tripping? I walk out of here exhausted, like emotionally beaten after some of these nights."

"And the voice just goes on and on," David said, dancing.

"On and on. We have to stand all alone emotionally here and we survive. And people think we're here because we can't handle things. They should only know how much we handle. That's how come so many of them can't handle the circuit."

"Right," David danced. "That's why so many of them leave after a little while. Not only can't they take it," he started.

"Which is fine," I interrupted.

"Which is *fine*," he said. "But then they criticize us and act as if we're being superficial by coming here."

"They accuse us of being trite," I danced sideways.

"And we are," he turned around and clapped.

"But it's hard," I said.

"It works me," David said emphatically. "Doubletime."

"This is work," I said turning around and clapping, doing his dance step to show I agreed.

I learn why they call it
The Holy Spirit

A couple of days later Mary sent me a letter, wrapped around three cassette tapes from the Club.

Her handwriting was parochial school penmanship gone to hell. "You stated that I opened your eyes to new vistas at The Holy Spirit," she began simply, "but you are wrong. You allowed yourself to see— one can look but not necessarily see. Someday when your mood is right go up to the balcony— alone or with a friend— sit back— do your ethyl as it does help you open the 3rd eye as it is known, and relax. Let it take you, not you direct it.

"In my first year at the Club (and till I caught hell for it) late at night or very early, depending on how you perceive things, I would lay back on the banquette and just gaze up, and if everything was right, could literally, if only for a short while, become one with the dome— the cosmos— eternity. Have rarely been able to do it in 2 years because of where my head has been at— not at peace with itself— but on the few occasions when I have fully let go— well, you claim you saw the occurrence if only in part."

You know I had to try that again. Then she sent me a bottle of ethyl and an orange rag. When I unwrapped it I found a gram of MDA inside. I figured getting an ethyl rag from Ethyl Mary is pretty official and I immediately mailed a thank-you note.

"Do you know what orange means?" she asked me later.

I shook my head. I could only remember what keys meant on the right and left; other than that, I just avoided people with handkerchiefs in their pockets altogether.

"Orange means anything goes," she explained archly.

David Walken and I took the bottle up to the balcony so we could sit in the bleachers and look through the top of the dome to the dance floor. In the darkness and given the expanse of the dome, its perforated metal was like a gauze and we could see the dancers moving in a filmy sort of way.

"That was very nice of Mary to give you a whole bottle for yourself," David said.

"Yeah, I thought so," I said as we settled in. I handed him the bottle and the rag and he bunched it up in a corner, soaked it with ethyl and then put it in his mouth. "David," I said, "I don't think you're doing it right." I took the free end of the rag that was hanging and did the same thing with it. We both sat there looking at the dome with an end of the rag in our mouths. As I got carried into the back and forth of the ethyl I started sticking my tongue in and out. I was acting out the back and forth, feeling that I had to.

"Harold, what are you *doing?*" David asked me. That brought me out of it. I took the rag out of my mouth and squirted it again. I handed the bottle to David so he could do it again too.

My drugs kicked in big time and I still was hearing the tone and counter-tone. Watching the dance floor lights, I focused on its center. My brain slowed visually and I looked down at the tree, now at a distance, and it became a bald figure standing in the middle and surrounded by writhing snake like movements. It was a primitive ceremony.

Anesthetized, I slowly handed David the bottle again. He accepted it mutely. I waited while he did more, staring down at the dance floor. Then I was relieved from the trace vision of the snakes adoring the bald figure, as I zoomed out and back and could look down at the dome from a really great distance now. David had one end of the rag in his mouth and I squirted out some more from the bottle and put the other end back in my mouth too. The dance floor looked like the globe with patterns of groups of dancers like continents, but they were shifting and moving as whole units. And then I was overcome with an understanding of the dance floor, and this was a confirmation of the idea I suspected on my first night: that it was one large being, and we were all part of it.

The primitivism of the idea and the understanding that it was no metaphor but reality blew me away and I jumped out of the bleacher and grabbed the metal grating in front of us. David must have thought I had lost my mind. I let go of the rag first, in case you're picturing me jumping up and pulling David with me by his teeth, and I just stood there and stared blankly at what I saw.

David immediately came out of it. "What is it?" he called urgently. "Harold, what's going on?"

"What's going on?" I was incredulous. I turned back to him and he was looking at me through his glasses like the reflection of my own consciousness. I looked back at him the same way. "What do you mean, 'What is it?'" I said. "You know what it is," I said, provoked. It didn't occur to me he hadn't seen the same thing.

"No, really," he said, sitting there looking at me, still too anesthetized to move. "Tell me."

"David," I said, recovering. I sat down again next to him. "Please. I will not be so gauche as to actually *talk* about it."

"You," he said, "are a queen with grand delusions."

"Come on," I said. We stood up carefully and made our way down the stairs with our arms straight down to judge the gravity. When we got down to the living room we found Robert and Tom.

"Hah, y'all," Tom said provocatively. "What's goin' on?"

"Hah," I said.

"Hah," David said. "Harold just had a fabulous experience in the dome but he won't tell anyone about it. Don't even ask him."

Robert laughed.

"What kind of fabulous experience did you have, Harold?" Tom asked. "I mean, don't tell me exactly. I wouldn't want to be as intrusive as David probably is," he went on. David's eyes and mouth opened and spread all over his face in indignation.

"Thanks, Tom," I said. "I knew you'd be gracious about it. Of course I can tell you. I just witnessed the dance floor which was in reality one large being of which we're all parts. Right away I understood about the spirit that's created from the feelings and action between beings."

Tom and David exchanged a look. "And that's what the Catholics mean by the mystical body of Christ that they teach about," I said. "That's probably also what they mean by The Holy Spirit which they teach is the feeling between one manifestation of God and another...and if that Holy Spirit is a conscious God entity, then that's what we've raised here. I've got it all figured out," I concluded. "That's God on the dance floor."

"Mary-stein," David said, "I'm sorry I asked." Robert smoked.

"Girl," Tom said.

"What's that supposed to mean?" I asked.

"Now, Harold Fenestere," he started.

"And I saw what you were just doing," I said. "You were talking to John Jr. and you zapped him."

Tom laughed and then he said, "Well, I had to."

"You know very well you're not supposed to," I said.

"I'm getting out of here," Robert said. "It's frightening to hear two sick people talk to each other."

"Now, you just hold on, Robert DiBlaisi," Tom said.

"This is impossible," Robert said.

"Knock it off, Tom," I said.

"This is impossible," Robert repeated. "I'm from Bensonhurst. I can't know the two sickest people in this Club."

"Darling," Tom said, "you introduced us."

"Would you like me to take over for a while?" David offered helpfully.

"You?" Robert asked hoarsely, taking the cigarette out of his mouth. "You're the one who started him on all this tonight. If I'd known, I never would've introduced you two either."

"I beg your pardon," David said indignantly as Tom took my arm and led me away.

"Come on," he said. "Let's leave them in confusion. Let's find Mary."

But Tom had to go unsatisfied that night because Mary disappeared for hours. "I was with Charles Bogard's friends," she explained the next night, Sunday. "He finally died last week. So I spent the whole night with them around three o'clock where Charles used to dance. We all had a good cry and then I said, 'OK, fellas, it's time to take out the fans.' So they took out their fans and I took out my ethyl and sat on the banquettes."

"Gosh," I said. "I'm sorry." This was when people were just beginning to die and we really didn't know all that many people who were sick.

"And I almost didn't make it tonight," she said. "I had a slave coming in from Boston but I managed to take care of him at home."

"That's good," I said. From upstairs I heard Robbie mixing into "Hold On." "Oh, not the old la-la song," I said. A middle-aged clone sitting next to her turned to me.

"You don't like that song?" he asked.

"Evan," Mary said, "This is Harold."

"How do you," I said. "I've been looking forward to meeting you."

"Mary's told me a lot about you too," he said formally. "Would you two excuse me?" he asked. "I'd really like to go dance to this song."

"Of course," Mary said. "See you later, Evan. Meet you at six o'clock."

"Listen, Mary," I said as her boyfriend hurried up the winding stairs to the second level. At the back of the Club queens were rushing up the other stairs two at a time. "You wouldn't want to go up to the balcony and do some more ethyl with me, would you?"

"Why not?" she said. "Lead the way."

"OK," I said leading us up the right side. I wondered if anyone saw us climbing up the winding iron stairs together. I also wondered what they might think we were doing.

"I hope no one sees me going up here with some twinkie," she said as we made our way around in the darkness.

"I'm not a twinkie," I said. "I'm twenty-seven years old."

"Big deal," she snorted, looking at me from the corner of her eye. Though I couldn't tell. When she faced me, all I could see was her oversized black glasses against her white countenance.

We sat down on the bleachers like I did with David the night before. What was I doing there every Saturday and Sunday? I remembered thinking at the beginning of the season I wasn't even going to come every weekend.

We settled in and started squirting ethyl on our rags. I felt like, look at me, I'm studying under Ethyl Mary. The first thing she did was take my rag from me and really douse it, like she did the night we met. Then we sat there staring at the dome with our rags in our mouths.

"You're forcing it," Mary said. "You can't force it."

"I don't want to miss anything," I whispered.

"You can't lead it," she said.

We kept doing it and I was thinking about Mary, about how she called me up one night and said, "This is Death"; and about how she's a Figure of Darkness. I wanted to send her positive vibes.

Mary went flying off her seat and landed on the floor. I was too anesthetized from the ethyl to even think about helping her. She looked up at me from the floor.

"Whew," she said. "Why don't you tell a girl when you're going to come up with something like that?"

"I wanted to surprise you," I said, pleased I'd been so successful.

"But you want to be my slave?" she asked.

"Your slave?" Her what? "Who said anything about being your slave?"

"Oops," she said, still on the floor as I watched her. "Excuse me. I must have gotten something wrong."

Not being able to stand it

After that I went home and slept for eighteen hours. By Tuesday evening I was able to handle the gym again.

Michael lay down on a mattress. He was one of the Diana People, one of the pretty and fashionable boys who attended her, along with Michael Arlene, Michael DuPres, Andrew Good, Edward Baker, David Leander, David Dear, Greg Wescott, Brian Owen and three other Davids, including David Walken. There were a few others whose names I never knew and who came and went within the season. No one had boyfriends.

David Walken and I were already positioned in the warm-up area. "Michael, I am just sick over what happened," I said. "I was affronted for you. It must have been horrible. Anthony actually shoving his jockstrap in your face. I don't blame you for throwing that locker at him."

"*I* didn't throw the locker," Michael said. His bright, black eyes and deep, straight hair made him playful and masculinely faun-like. "That Anthony creature knocked it over herself. One moment I was getting dressed and the next thing I knew Anthony was screaming something about I had knocked her filthy T-shirt on the floor and she grabs a jock strap and starts coming at me."

"It must have been awful for you," I said.

"Awful? It was disgusting. Naturally I jumped back and unfortunately the lockers behind me went slamming backwards and hit some poor asshole on the other side. I don't care, it was her own fault."

"Michael," David intoned languidly from his pallet, "whatever did you do to Lenny last week-end?"

"Yeah," I said. "What was she talking about anyway?"

"*I* didn't do it," Michael said. "Barry Albertson did. But I just couldn't stand it anymore either."

David leaned up for a moment, propped up on his elbows. "Stand what?" he asked.

"The way Lenny always goes after the new faces, and *gets them,*" I explained to David.

"Why, what's happened?" David asked, leaning back down again and closing his eyes. He lay still.

Michael stood up. "I was with Barry Albertson," he explained. "And we met this new kid, a very nice young fellow, who'd never been there before. He was only twenty.

"We had the nicest conversation and Barry and I decided he was a nice fellow. Well, don't you know, later who did we see dancing with him but Lenny? And I thought, no, I won't have this. I just cannot have this. So I said to Barry, I said, 'Look, Lenny's got another one. Something has to be done.'"

Michael laughed and threw his hands up. "And Barry went right up to where they were dancing, took the kid aside and said to him, 'The person you are dancing with is socially unacceptable, you cannot be seen with him, and he is notorious. And he is potentially unhealthy.'"

Michael laughed again, his long black lashes closing against his tanned skin. His eyes opened again and he looked at us playfully. "That should stop him." He actually slapped both his thighs.

There was a pause. "That was a horrible thing to do to Lenny," I said then. "No matter how trying it is to see him always preying on the new faces."

"But how did Lenny know what you said about him?" David asked.

"*Because,*" Michael turned to David. "This kid turned to Lenny and *told* him."

"That was awful," Bobby said. He joined us on the floor.

"I know," Michael said. "Can you imagine. He actually *told* Lenny." Michael slapped his hands against his thighs again. "That's what I get for doing a good deed." He lay down again on his mattress.

"Michael," I said, "you cannot do that to Lenny."

"Well, I don't see why not," Michael said. "I felt it had to be done."

"Michael," I said, "I know how annoying it is to see Lenny going after every new face that walks onto the circuit. I find it just as galling as you do. But these things take care of themselves, and I have yet to see one of these new faces not catch on by himself. And Lenny's as entitled as anyone else," I added fairly.

"He's a psychotic," Michael said from the floor.

"I know he is, but you can't do this again. Once is funny, but you can't do it again."

"How about once in a while?" Michael asked.

"No," I said.

"Well, alright," Michael said. He settled into position. We lay there in silence for a while.

"Michael," I said from my mattress. He looked over at me. "OK," I said. "You can do it for parties."

A blind date with a sensitive boy

"DRUGS & DISCO," I wrote in like, my fourth personal ad in the *Native*. Dancing at The Holy Spirit precluded any cruising so I looked for alternative methods. "Do you like to dance? GWM 27 slim 5'7" 140 br/br cleanshaven seeks similar boyfriend for dating and sleeping close. Anarchists encouraged."

This yielded nothing; or no one memorable. Then I answered an ad, something about a slim cleanshaven twenty-seven-year-old. Made-to-order.

"Did you notice some of the other personals in the same column as yours?" I wrote him. "Where do these people get words like 'non-pretentious'? Where does someone get the balls to write a thing like 'Here's your chance'? You sound like an appealing fellow (like me). I'm 27, 5'7" and 140 lbs. Is that slim? I noticed you avoided exact statistics; do you have a thing about them? Like you mentioned, I'm not a yuppie either, and I don't mean that defensively the way I imagine self-deceiving fascist capitalists talk in Conran's. (I realize I have a problem.) I am, in fact, downwardly mobile and have, in one generation, brought my family back fifty years to the Lower East Side, where I am quite happy (if a little fearful) in a tenement studio. What about you?

Have I talked too much? If you'd like to meet and talk in person, my number is 533-0527."

(Signed)

"Harold Fenestere"

I know it was smug, but it got a response. The whole idea was to meet guys, and I thought it had to be done in a way that would have nothing to do with The Holy Spirit Dance Club. But this turned out to have a lot to do with it.

This fellow called me, which is the point of this part of the story. He sounded charming on the phone, though I've noticed there are differences in the impressions people make (1) by describing themselves in writing, (2) by how they sound over the phone, and (3) by what they're like in person. I'm an expert at this. We spoke for almost an hour. I was defrosting my freezer anyway.

So I was in for one more. Sitting in a Japanese restaurant on Avenue A, right after work, wearing my father's harris tweed jacket, I was remembering a couple of other blind dates when I agreed to meet the guy for dinner instead of just a fast drink. They were both against my initial inclinations and they were both great first dates followed by horrific second ones. The kind where you wonder where your mind was the first time. The kind where you wish you could just get up and leave.

I looked around at the grey and black decor, the exotic flowers, which seemed ubiquitous that year. The waiters were either Japanese monks or just dressed like them, with belted tunics and shaved heads. This guy appeared with one of the monks behind him. "Hi," he said as I stood up. "I'm Daniel."

The first things I noticed were (1) he looked lean and muscular, and was handsome. (2) He had lied about being twenty-seven and (3) his hair was colored. It was dark brown, highlighted with some product so new it probably wouldn't be prevalent for a while. His clothes had that avant look too. I'm suspicious of people who lie about their age and change their hair color.

"Hi," I answered as we shook hands and sat down. "I'm Harold Fenestere."

He actually smiled shyly and he said, "You know, I've never done this before."

I made a face. "Not that I'm a tired queen who's been around," I said, "but I never believe that someone hasn't done something before. Usually they turn out to be pretty good at it. Quite in control of things."

He laughed, confirming my thoughts: he wasn't shocked by a shocking statement. Please, sister, I felt like saying, but I wanted to hear what he had to say.

"Really," he said. "I have this puerile interest in personals and I wanted to run a position and copy test." For a four line ad? "I've been doing this for a while," he went on. "It started when I was living in Charleston."

"You're from Charleston?" I interrupted him. "Do you know Jerry Harris? He's from Charleston."

"No," he said. "But when I lived there, I used to do the same thing, just to test special positioning. I wanted to see if those Personal Ads of the Week pulled any better than in-column ads. You might be interested to know they do worse," he went on. As he cut his food I noticed his hands were both strong and delicate; as he talked I noticed his eyes were brown and soft. "And I've gotten actually about a thousand letters over the years. Yours was such an exception I had to answer it," he said as the waiter brought our order, not particularly deferentially, for a monk.

"In other words," I said, "to titillate yourself, you've been running ads that you didn't really intend to answer, except maybe." I put down my drink. "You dangled yourself in front of a classified readership's noses, through some sort of printed distance so you could get off on it. As for mine being the exception," I concluded, "I'm just gay enough to have no hesitation believing it but, honey, I am suspicious of gratuitous praise." I looked at my food. It was moving. I pushed it aside.

He sat back in his chair, holding onto his drink. His hair color seemed to have gotten more artificial. Maybe it was a wig. Then he ran his hands through it.

"It's true," he said. I couldn't believe how quickly he snapped. "I did only place the ad as a test. But when I got your letter I showed it to my lover and we both agreed I should call you."

Your who? I thought. This was frank. The waiter came by with the check, and I let him pick it up.

Not that I've been around a hundred years, but doesn't it always seem that when you meet a nice looking, sensitive guy, and that should be the tip-off, nobody gets past twelve or so with sensitivity completely intact, that there's something he's not telling you? Like (1) he's just broken up with someone, (2) he's really more into some other type or (3) he's moving away in a couple of days.

This guy being married was a new one on me. I know it's the most obvious one but I had just helped an old woman across the street the day before for the first time in my life. I felt like I was getting around to the few firsts I had left.

I didn't know what to do since I'd already invested time (after all), compared to when you meet somebody who tells you he's married and you move on, so I suggested we go somewhere for a drink. I could see him congratulating himself.

At the bar I brought up the subject of his apartment. "How big is it?" I asked.

"It's seven rooms," he said.

"Seven," I answered. "Gosh, I live in one. That's great."

"Yeah," he said. "It's really nice having so much space. We'd like to move, but where else could we find an affordable apartment even half that size?"

"Yeah. I know your problem," I said leaning forward. I put my hand under my chin as I spoke. "And I think your problem is that you are actually standing there and referring, parenthetically no less, to your lover, as if there were nothing wrong with your going on a date when you're married."

He ran his hands through his hair, a calculated gesture of appeasement. "Well, yes," he said, "I thought you knew I was married."

"Daniel," I said, "how the hell would I know you were married unless you told me? When you mentioned it over dinner it was the first I heard of it. How dare you place an ad in the newspaper so you can cheat on your lover? You don't even have the honesty to acknowledge your purpose." The bartender leaned away from us and switched off a tape. The piano player was sitting down.

"Harold," he said, "honestly, I didn't think it mattered."

"Of course it didn't matter to you. You were out to suit yourself. Don't you know what false pretenses are?"

"But if we're both interested in the same thing, what difference does it make?" I admit I could've walked out at that point, but what ran platitudinously through my head was, in for a penny, in for a pound.

"Let me point something out to you," I said. "We are not both in this for the same thing. You are in this to get laid. I am single. I am in this to get laid and possibly to pursue a relationship with the person I have sex with.

"Further," I said. With me there's always a further. In case you haven't noticed. "Further, what do you think? That the whole rest of the world is just waiting to get laid, and that anyone, single or married, with options to offer or none at all, can just come by and pick what he wants? Wake up and smell the coffee. This is 1984." The piano player was singing now and this piano bar stuff was really rankling me. "Are we all physical commodities? Still? Maybe to you guys who came out when that's what was done. How old are you anyway?"

"Thirty-one."

"And what color is your hair?"

"What do you mean?" he asked, running his hands through his hair again.

"Nevermind," I said. "Look, here's the point. Even if we are physical commodities on an open market, we have the prerogative of deciding that, rather than letting some married person come by and presume.

"And another thing," I said, "I don't like to invest my time in married people and I don't care for the politics of such an unequal meeting."

"OK, listen," he cracked again. "There's more."

"More?"

"I'll tell you the truth. Really. Remember when I told you I lived in Charleston and you asked if I knew Jerry Harris? Well, he's my lover."

"Gerard was the lover who also read my letter and agreed you should call me."

"Right. He suggested it, actually." Daniel's eyes animatedly took in the room then came back to me. "He said he knew you, though not well, and he really couldn't answer for what you were like physically but he said you were a very nice person."

I laughed at that one.

"I guess you're ready to kill me," he said.

"That's silly," I said, thinking I might, perhaps, invite him back to my apartment and bite his dick off or something. "Besides," I went on, "you might infer from such a developed and entrenched personal philosophy that I'm not unused." I paused. "Would you like to have a drink at my place?"

"Well, sure," he said, and had the grace to appear bewildered.

OK, so far this is nothing more than a tale of coincidence and unlikely occurrences in which (1) this guy places an ad that I answer and (2) from all the replies, he answers only mine and (3) his lover is someone I know.

We walked the couple of blocks to my apartment. I unlocked the door on the one room and held it open for him. "Oh, this is very nice," he said, the way people say when they mean, "Well, this is OK if you really want to live this way, but I could never."

"I like the palm tree," he said.

"A gift from a madman," I said, watching him take in the cracked wall, the water stain on the ceiling. The only furniture I had were a sofa and a futon mattress. Books were piled against one wall. "I like it. It's nice and spare."

"It reminds me of a garret space I saw in Brooklyn Heights once," Daniel said, taking in the gates across one window, the view of the tenement courtyard from the other.

Oh, brother, I thought. "Speaking of Brooklyn Heights," I said to make small talk, which I was pretty much dying for by now. "I was just talking today with a friend there. She was telling me about this ghost in her apartment, and she said it fucks her." (My telling Daniel this is random occurrence #4.)

Well, this seemed to be his topic (#5). "I wouldn't be so frivolous about that," he said. "You should tell your friend to be careful."

"What do you mean?" I said. "I believe her. I think it's possible."

"Oh, I think it's possible too," he said. "You're talking to a believer. I believe in spirit forces, and I believe that any spirit force that makes itself felt by physically imposing itself on someone is hostile, and dangerous. It's expressing anger. It's acting as violently as it can."

"I get the point," I said. "I'll call her tomorrow and tell her to knock it off."

"I'd tell her a bit more than that," he went on. "Explain to her what I just told you, and tell her that any spirit that's kind would not make her feel its presence. At the most, it might bring a warm, pleasant feeling to a person it had been close to."

I scowled and sat back in the divan, pulling a blanket over myself. I have to admit I was interested, considering what I was noticing at The Holy Spirit (#6). "Listen," I said. "I have to tell you some things. You know The Holy Spirit Dance Club?" Of course he did; every gay person knew about it. "Well, there's something I don't usually mention to people on first dates either. I go there every weekend," I said, waiting for him to draw the usual conclusions about sex, drugs and general licentiousness.

"And I've been getting a real education there," I said. "I walked into that Club a few months ago with no particular belief system. I wasn't an atheist, I just didn't believe in anything." I stopped for a second; this was the first time I was articulating all the energy theories I was trying to work out there.

"And anyway, since I've been going there and noticing all these things about energy, I've been thinking...well, actually, I think this with some certainty, that once energy gets created, it exists. It just exists forever, and once it's released it has to go somewhere." He nodded seriously, but I was probably being serious too. "I've seen energy get created and it like, shoots out. I've seen what happens to it and I know what it looks like."

"Harold," he said, folding his hands under his chin. But his brown eyes were still soft and he was friendlike. "I've been dealing with energy forces since I was a kid. I even thought everyone could see them. I didn't know they couldn't, and it made trouble for me. So you're not alone.

"I've seen all sorts of things," he went on. "There are good forces and there are others that are accumulations of anger and hostility that are so powerful that they stay around even after the person generating them has died. These are the kinds of things you have to watch out for, Harold," he said, sitting back and crossing his legs.

Oh, I thought, and what about married people? I sat back farther, pulling the blanket around me. Alluring, huh? "I've seen monstrous things ever since I was a child," he said. Yeah, I'll bet. Then I thought maybe I was carrying this posture too far. I'll be fair. I'll relax.

"I've had things barking at me in the dark," he said. Relax? By this time I was huddled in the corner of the sofa with the blanket pulled up to my chin. Remember I'm a sissy.

I'd heard enough. "So what's Jerry been up to lately?" I asked.

"Oh, he's been dating some kid," Daniel confided.

"See, here's the truth," he said. More truth was coming. "We have this open relationship, and Jerry has been dating this kid who I absolutely cannot stand."

"And you haven't been 'dating' anyone," I said. "And you and Gerard want you to even the score."

"Well, yeah," he said flatteringly.

When he left I thought, here this guy came out of nowhere through these random events (approximately six of them) and, knowing things I didn't, called me up and made a date with me. He met me and used me to accomplish some private purpose. Then I had to listen while he talked about his marriage, as if I could have stood one more cliche at this point, and expiated his guilt about being there with me, which was even more flattering. And he told me ghost stories, besides, and spooked me.

Sleeping with the light on

You'd think that this was enough for one weekend but this was only Friday night.

Saturday I was indulging myself in feeling used when my mother called: my dog died. Anyhow, I realize now, while I'm writing this, that my dog is connected to this weekend's story. This left me exposed and probably kind of tautened my sensitivity. It made me more open.

Saturday night I went to The Holy Spirit, and you know what kind of experience that is, what it opens your mind to, with the drugs, the physical activity of dancing, being without sleep, and just the whole bizarre setting there. After only a short layover Sunday afternoon, Robert and I went to a drug dealer's party and I drank test tube in a drug punch for the first time since the night two years ago when I ran out of The Holy Spirit at two in the morning.

Sunday afternoon Robert slept over, so he'd have some place to crash after the drug dealer's party. After the drugs and exposure, I couldn't sleep; I was just lying there in the dark looking up at the shadows of the bamboo shades and the fire escape on the ceiling. Robert rolled over.

"I want a valium," he mumbled.

"Forget it," I said. "We don't have enough to come down with."

"Huh?" he said, sitting up. "Oh, my God," he said seeing the shadows on the ceiling. "Snakes!"

I rolled over too. "Forget it," I said again into my pillow. "I told you we only have enough valium for Monday."

"What are you talking about?" he said. His nostrils engorged and his sinuses flushed noisily upward. "What are those *snakes* on the ceiling?"

"Honey," I said, "those are shadows."

"Oh."

"Can we go back to sleep now?"

"OK." He half ingested his sinuses again.

I put my head in the pillow and he started in again. "I want a valium," I heard in a clear monotone.

"Robert," I said with finality. "I told you, no valium."

"What *are* you talking about?" he screeched. He sat up and looked at me.

"You keep asking for a valium. No valium."

"I do not," he insisted. "I don't even want a valium."

I just looked at him.

"Well, OK," he said. "Now that you mention it."

Then I started to figure out what was going on. When I went back to the Club later that night I was still wired. Mary was watching me because she pulled me aside. "Boy," she said, "you're really picking up on people all over the place, aren't you?" and she wasn't referring to pick-ups as in meeting boys, and that surprised me since I hadn't told her about any of this stuff.

"Yeah," I said. "This is weird. Why didn't you warn me? Do you realize I've been so impolite as to tell people what I've been hearing?"

She just laughed. "How could I know you were ready?" she asked.

So think about what I'm like by Monday: very strung out. Is it any surprise that I went into work on Tuesday morning and said what I said?

When I went to bed Monday night, when I turned off the light in that apartment, there was something there. As soon as I turned off the light I felt it and I got back up and turned the light on. I could feel it and I could see it. The air was moving with it.

I remembered what Daniel told me. He said that negative forces have to be met strongly and if they're trying to harm you, you have to meet them head on.

I lay back down with the light on. Are you picturing this, me, lying on a mattress on the floor in a one room tenement apartment with the light on, looking around in terror? I thought, I'm going to have to deal with this, so deal with it. I figured if I have to sleep with the light on, I'll do it.

Well, eventually I started to fall asleep and that's when this thing moved in because I started to get that feeling like when you're in bed and you're almost paralyzed and you can't get up and you feel like you'd better because if you don't now, you never will. Daniel told me about this too; he said this was transient, hostile spirits trying to inflict themselves on you when you're resting and your brainwaves are lower.

I woke up and shook it off me. Then I tried to sleep again. This time I made it for a while longer, I think, because when it woke me up again I was in a deeper sleep. But this time it was flooding through me and my eyes shot open and I jumped up and stood on the futon and clutched at my hair. The hem of my blanket was torn and had gotten wrapped around my throat and I was caught in it. I frantically detangled myself from the cover in a release of terror. Then I felt myself free from the feeling in the room. I watched my own energy push it out under the door. The air was suddenly empty and clear.

Later I woke up again and the vibes in the air were thick and wiry again, but this time it felt so comforting I let it calm me down. I figured I needed it and I'd take my chances. It spoke to me low. But anyway, this is what happened that night, and I went into work the next morning and said I hadn't slept well because I had a ghost in my apartment.

My boss looked at me across her desk. She was my age, she took drugs, and she was trying to be sympathetic. "Harold," she said finally, "you realize this is very difficult for me. You know I have a hard time believing these things."

I know that, I thought. You wouldn't be general manager of this division if you didn't. But I respected her pragmatism. "Look at it this way," I tried. "Whether it happened or not, I went through it."

"That's true," she said. We lit a joint and sat back. When I went home that night I opened my apartment door very carefully, but everything was cool. I threw out the ripped blanket right away, though.

It comes back to a twinkie

I stood with the director of the gym against one of the banquettes on the lower floor, the one below the dance floor. His hair was cut militarily short except in back where a thick krishna crop grew out all the way from his crown to his nape, like a muscle, like the rest of his body. He smoked a cigarette while he lounged against the three levels of the banquette.

A young boy passed. "Hey, uh, excuse me," Bobby called out. He put his cigarette out as the boy turned but didn't come any closer.

"Can I, uh, talk with you a minute?" Bobby asked him, turning back from the ashtray.

The kid came closer. "My name's Scott," he said.

"Nice to meet you, Scott," Bobby said. "This is my friend, Harold. You were here last Saturday, weren't you?"

"It was my first night," the kid said.

"I know," Bobby said. "So, uh, listen, I heard you weren't too nice to Lenny."

"The weirdest things happened that night," the kid said.

"Listen," Bobby said. "Weird things happen here. Let me explain a couple of things for you. You're new here, and you don't know too many people, right?"

He didn't wait for the kid to answer. "So you can't afford to offend people, since you don't

97

really know who's who or who's friends with whom. Now, as far as Lenny is concerned, the next time something like that happens, you *don't* turn to the person and repeat what you've just heard about them. You don't hurt someone's feelings.

"Even Lenny's. The next time your friends come up to you when you're with someone and tell you things, if you decide to listen to every-thing that's said to you by people you don't know, you don't have to tell the other person what you heard. This is a polite society. You just say, 'Excuse me, I have to join my friends' or 'It was nice meeting you, I have to go now.'"

"I guess I might not have handled it right," the kid said.

"That's alright," Bobby said. "You didn't know."

The archetype reveals his desire

"And then right in the middle of this trip Bobby says to me, 'I'm sorry about everything I said about you, it's just that everyone else got me started.'"

"You're kidding," I said.

"No, I'm not," Tom said.

"Well," I said, "I would say it was incredible but someone else said something similar to me the other day, something that just astounded me. I don't remember how the subject came up but I said something like, 'Who would ever want to know all the horrible things everyone else says about one? Who would even tell one what everyone else says?' And Tim O'Brien said, 'Bobby Cantor would.' Evidently Bobby came right up to Tim in the gym, that very morning actually, and said something like, 'I heard that you and Mark have been replaced by Barry and Michael as Ed and Brian's friends.'"

"This is more serious than I thought," Tom said.

"Wait," I said. "There's more. The worse part is that Tim absolutely fixated on who had said that to Bobby. He kept saying, 'I just want to know who said that to him.'"

"My God," Tom said low in his throat. "Well," he continued, "there's more to my story, too. So we go up to the dance floor fucked up and he introduces me to someone as the person he wants to do the autopsy on him when he dies."

"He didn't."

"He most certainly did. And the worst part is, I don't even know if he knew the person or not."

"What do you mean?"

"I mean, can you imagine if he just walked up to some complete stranger and introduced me as the person he wanted to do the autopsy on him when he died?"

"Tom," I said, "if that were the case it would be pathological."

"That's right," Tom pronounced.

"Tom," I said again, "that would mean he was actually dangerous."

"That's exactly what I think is possible," Tom said. "He might kill one of us. We don't know."

"Oh, my God," I said.

"Body Rock" was playing through the ceiling of the dome. "There's something else I have to tell you," Tom began. "I'm obsessed with Robert DiBlaisi."

"You're not serious," I said.

"I am," he said. "You don't understand."

"You're right," I told him. "I don't. What could you see in an Italian-American from Brooklyn?"

"Not just Brooklyn," Tom said. "Bensonhurst. Robert's from Bensonhurst, and I think Bensonhurst is the center of the universe."

"You must be kidding," I corrected him. "Bensonhurst isn't the center of the universe, though it's close. The Holy Spirit is the center of the universe. I thought you knew that."

"Oh, no," he said. "It's Bensonhurst. Any place that grows them like that has to be the center. I can't believe what I've seen there."

"What have you seen in Bensonhurst?" I asked.

"Harold," he explained patiently, "all my life I dreamed of a certain type, a rugged man. You know, the longshoreman type."

"The garbage man type," I said.

"Right," he said.

"You mean, like *Welcome Back, Kotter?*" I asked him.

"Yeah," he said patiently, even though I was dragging this out. I thought it a simple matter that anyone who'd perform an autopsy after the Black Party would enjoy protracting a painful subject.

"Did you know," I asked him, "that Robert went to the same high school as in *Welcome Back, Kotter?* He went to New Utrecht."

"Listen, Harold," Tom said, "do you want me to explain this to you or not?

"Now," he went on, "when I lived in Texas, I always dreamed of someone like Robert DiBlaisi. He typifies my ideal. But I never thought such a person actually existed. And when I came to New York, I found him.

"Italian-Americans from Brooklyn," he continued, "are my perfect type. And Robert DiBlaisi is the quintessential Italian-American."

"It doesn't even bother you that he wouldn't know what 'quintessential' means?"

"No, that's what I love most about him," Tom said.

"Well," I said sort of resignedly, "if that's what you want."

"That's what I want," he said pointedly as if something had been resolved.

"But what do you want with him?"

"Oh," he said and at this point I thought he was having a serious break with reality. "I intend to have a meaningful, lifelong relationship with him. I've already bought a gold chain so I can wear one, too."

"But Tom, look at him," I said. "If Robert DiBlaisi looks like the quintessential anyone, it's the quintessential heterosexual. He's got to be putting a lot of effort into that. He's not happy about being gay." OK, so I was lying about one of my oldest friends in the world. But I knew I had to put Tom off Robert's track. "And anyone who's that unhappy about being gay," I went on, "who puts all that effort into acting fully the opposite of what he is, must have a lot of hostility. I wouldn't want to be around when he loses control of that."

"Oh, I would," Tom said.

"Tom," I said, "he could split you in two."

"Do you think so?" he asked. He was confirming every dark motive I ever ascribed to him. "Gosh, I sure hope so. That's what I came to New York for.

"And now that I'm here," he finished, "I want to enter into a conjugal life with someone who is the very model of my nemesis and who is likely to actually kill me in the hostile act of love."

"Tom," I said but fortunately Santos came by.

Speaking of nemeses

"Tell me," Santos said to Tom. "In your line of work, do you ever perform autopsies on people with engorged erections?" I was appalled.

"Oh, why, yes," Tom said and sat back in the banquette, clearly ready to settle into this topic.

"Tell me about it," Santos said with just the clipped suggestion in his accent of La Fangito. He was wearing a classic black suit and his black glasses. He took them off for this conversation and peered closely at Tom.

"Why, sometimes they bring them in and they're so swollen, one was fifteen inches long and three inches in diameter." Santos looked at him, his mouth open in horror. I was disgusted. I moved down one level on the banquettes.

"There's Julio," I said as Santos' friend walked carefully up to the banquettes. "I love your jacket," I told him.

"Thank you," he said deeply as he slowly sat down, his black jacket carefully in place over his body stocking.

"Doesn't Julio look good?" Santos asked.

"Yes, I was just about to say so," I said.

And, "He sure does," Tom agreed.

Julio, with his dark eyes and his eye shadow, looked at us silently.

"Julio and I have been hanging out in straight bars lately. And we've been making out very well, haven't we, Julio?"

"Straight bars?" I asked. "What could you want from straight bars?"

"Why, rough trade, it used to be called. I wouldn't touch none of these sick faggots. You know," Santos went on, "I was once married to a doctor. How I loved to hear him talk of autopsies," he reminisced.

"Was he a pathologist also?" Tom asked.

"No, dear," Santos said. "An oncologist. He and all his cancer loving friends used to come over and we would have the grandest dinner parties. All in one room in the West Village."

"Are you sure he wasn't a pathologist as well?" Tom asked. "Sometimes oncologists are."

"He was pathological," Julio interjected distinctly.

"Yes, he was, unfortunately," Santos said. "But it was a fun time. Now Julio and I must be off," he said.

"Goodbye, Julio," I said.

"Goodbye," he intoned throatily as they evanesced.

Tom and I sat there in silence. "Golly," Tom said finally.

I got up and went up to the dance floor.

"What's eating you?" Tom asked, following me up there.

"Nothing," I said. "Do you want some ethyl?"

"Well, sure," he said. We stepped into the moving people and started dancing in place while we squirted the ethyl onto our rags and stuck the ends in our mouths.

We did it again and I watched while he tripped. When I was sure he was gone, I stepped close up to his face and I said, "You monster, I know what you're doing here."

"What do you mean?" He opened his eyes.

"Look," I said. "I know what's going on here. Or at least I have some idea. Something's going on here, you'll admit."

"Yes, I'll admit it," he said seriously. We were still moving from the waist down. I hated talking on the dance floor, but I wanted this discussed.

"Something's going on here. We're leading up to something, right?"

"Right," he nodded. "The end of the world."

I laughed. "And you and I couldn't be more opposed, could we?"

"Well." He was confused for a moment.

"Yet we're here, clearly to square off for something. I've listened to you talk, Tom," I said. "I know what you're up to. Something is about to happen here and it is you, here, to confront me, in an attempt to destroy me."

"That's right," he said. "I am here to destroy the absolute being of your soul."

I laughed and hit him on the shoulder. "Well, as long as that's out of the way. As long as we've admitted it." I danced off the floor, and trounced happily down the stairs.

And there was Mary. "Well, hi," she said.

"Hi," I said quickly, swinging down next to her.

"Yes?" she said.

"Mary," I leaned close, "what's going on here?"

"What are you talking about?" she asked me politely.

"I mean, have you noticed a few things about the structure here?"

"Such as?"

"Such as things being constructed in threes? Like there are three steps up to the dance floor?"

"There are seven," she said.

"Oh, no," I said. "I'm sure there are three."

"Trust me," she said. "You see these black glasses? There are seven stairs. I've counted them," she said decisively.

"Well," I said, "seven is a significant number, isn't it?"

"What are you getting at?" she asked inexpressively.

"Something's going on here. This place exists for something."

"Yeah," she said. "For dancing. And to take drugs."

"But what about what we saw with the ethyl?" I said.

"Do you think everyone else sees what you see?" she asked truculently.

"Well, sure," I answered.

"They don't. It's a *disco*," she added forbiddingly.

"OK," I said. I could let it drop for now.

Two queers cross Mary without considering the implications

"I have just taken enough downs to kill an army," Mary announced over the phone. "And I am going to sleep."

"Do you mind if I come over?" I asked.

"If you insist," she said tolerantly. "It's apartment 2D."

When I got there, she was extremely pale, but someone who hasn't been up in the daytime in almost ten years is likely to be pale. She was wearing a housedress and her long hair was loose and hanging behind her back. Her dark glasses hid her eyes.

"Come in, sit down," she said. "Would you like some ice tea?"

"Um, no," I said, falling down into a large cushion, since I had run most of the ten blocks between us. Her cat, Holden Caulfield, jumped into my lap.

"Thank you for coming," she said formally.

"Why did you take all those pills?" I asked.

"Why not? I've had it. I've had it with everyone from that Club. Everyone. And I'm going to kill Miguel. I'm going to make him sorry he ever interfered with my life.

"That muscle queen," she continued. "That self-proclaimed top who's got nothing going for him but his capped teeth, and even those he didn't pay for, Evan did.

"You know I've been sleeping with Evan?" she went on. "The whole thing was a nice, adult arrangement. We all know each other, we're all part of the same circles. Evan and I just happened to fall into bed one day and we had a very good time. Well, Miguel didn't like that.

"I was making no attempt to interfere with their relationship. It was just Evan and me, playing, once a week. We decided, Evan and I will play, Miguel has other playmates. It was working fine, but Miguel couldn't stand it. He forced Evan to break it up. I'm going to kill Miguel."

"Mary," I said, "maybe it wouldn't be such a hot idea to actually kill him. You know that could bring on more trouble than it would be worth."

"Oh, it would be worth it," she said. "But maybe you're right. Maybe I can think of something a little more devastating." She picked up the black rotary telephone from the floor and put it in her lap. She cradled the phone between her shoulder and her ear as she flipped the pages in her phone book. "I can never remember numbers," she said. She reached her tongue out to her nose while she dialed.

"Hello, Miguel?" she said. "You know who this is. Is Evan there? Oh, he's not, is he? Well, give him a message for me. Tell him that you and he can expect a phone call from the management of The Holy Spirit this weekend. Your membership's being cancelled...Because I'm friends with one of the investors, that's why...When you and Evan get to the Club this weekend, your money will be refused, and you will be escorted to your lockers, so you can clean them out....

"I'm sorry, Miguel, it's out of my hands. It wasn't even my idea. I didn't want it to happen.

108

I was telling my friend about how upset I am over the way you and Evan have acted and he insisted on doing this...I told you, I tried to talk him out of it. I begged him. Unh-unh, he refused...No, there's nothing that can be done. Yeah. Good-bye."

She hung up the phone and looked at me. "How's that?" she asked.

"Too fucking much," I said. The phone rang.

"Hello?" she answered. "No, Evan," she said. "That's not true. Your wife got it wrong. I did not have you kicked out of The Holy Spirit. In fact, I tried to prevent it, but it's too late. Apparently, I have friends who care. Like the friend who's with me now...Nevermind who it is. What's important is that you have treated me terribly and now you're paying for it."

She hung up again. "You know," she said, "it always amazes me how willing people are to expose their underbellies right after they've made an enemy."

"Well, good for you," I said. "You took care of them. But shouldn't we do something about you? What about all those pills you took?"

"Don't worry about it," she said. "I just took ten or twenty of whatever downs I had lying around. I've taken more than that just to come down on a Saturday night."

"Are you sure you'll be alright?"

"Perfectly," she said. She tapped her eye with her fingernail. It was glass, and she did it again. "See you tomorrow night," she said as she tapped it.

The White Light

The next night I was walking up the black iron stairs to the dance floor, while the people in their familiar outfits travelled around and carried on. This was probably the only disco in the world where people not only shamelessly showed up at the same place every week, they wore the same clothes each time, too, the development of the most comfortable outfit to dance in subordinated to any need for diversity in fashion. It was five or so in the morning and high energy was peaking. A group of fan dancers arrived on the other side. They took a moment to set up and then they took their silver fans out of their back pockets and, like aviary creatures, began to flutter them.

I looked into the crowd. One man walked serenely by trailing a man on a leash. Another man with a fan auspiciously and quickly entered at nine o'clock as "Holding Out for a Hero" drove the floor. Then the tree in the center of the floor rose slowly from its low position; it rose up gracefully and steadily as the dancers there moved out of the way.

The Diana People arrived and settled their place near eleven o'clock, one boy turning to the banquettes to put out his cigarette as Diana chose two others to dance with. The Japanese woman danced by and I was pretty sure she was looking at me. Then the Diana People descended on her to kiss her hello.

110

Tom Sanders came up and stood beside me, wearing his rhinestone armband like a shield. He looked distressed. "Hello, Harold," he said grimacing. He held a cigarette to his mouth.

"Hi, Tom," I said. "What's the matter?"

"Aw, nuthin," he said, and kept walking. An oversized hick in overalls walked dumbly behind him. Well, I thought, I see Tom has found one of his ideal men. I hurried after him.

"What are you doing?" I asked him.

"Harold, help me get rid of this guy," he said miserably.

"Why?" I said. "He looks like your type."

"He is, but I can't get rid of him. He's been following me around all night."

I turned and looked at the guy again. "I can't believe we're just talking about him like this," I said.

"That's *nothing*," Tom said making his letters ring. "We haven't even spoken yet. He just came up to me while I was sitting downstairs and put that big arm around me."

"Well, I should think you'd like that," I said.

"I *did*," he said. "For about a minute. Now I want to get rid of him."

"Pick Up The Phone" mixed in an abrupt downbeat into "Dancing In The Dark." There was an immediate evacuation by every clone on the floor. I looked at the dance floor and saw all the people moving; everything was starting to sparkle and then it segued into a cloudlike movement as it shifted counterclockwise. I watched the dance floor slope downward and I wondered if it was really doing that all the time and we could just see it better now. I looked back at Tom. He looked at me out of the corner of his eye.

111

Tom needs authority, I figured, which is probably why he needs to be dominated. "Listen, boy," I said roughly. "Here you have the opportunity to get what you want. Now, take it. What do you think, we whipped up this frenzy for nothing? We're caught in this vortex," I said watching everything go around. The dance floor was still sloping from all the drugs we took. "And we're in it to make things happen. Now, you take this farmboy home with you and have him fuck you."

"'Farmboy,'" he said low in his throat, slinking away under the light beams. "Probably the reason he hasn't spoken is because he's from Long Island."

I sat down on the banquette. Himiko danced out of the crowd and came and sat beside me, looking straight out. Then I turned to look at her as she turned to me. "Hi," I said. "My name's Harold." I put out my hand.

"Hi, Harold," she said simply. She shook my hand. "Himiko."

"Yes," I said. "I know."

She smiled. "Yes, I already heard your name too. Here, I have a present for you." She stood up and reached her hand into her jeans and took something from her wallet which she handed me: a one-inch square picture of a ray of white light. "It's the light from the star machine." She touched my head in a modified gesture of familiarity. "But don't tell anyone," she added.

"Gosh," I said. "Thanks."

Then she put a cigarette to her lips, lit it deftly, winked and was off.

The Great Conundrum

One night that week I tried something. It was early evening, the city seemed quiet; at least from my view of the other tenements it did. I sat down on the floor; I know, I should buy some chairs. I sprayed the ethyl on my ethyl rag and put it in my mouth, and with no dance floor to look at, I let my vision go. What interested me is what I heard: it wasn't the grinding disco beat of the music you always hear in the background. I didn't have any music on, and what I heard was words, a sentence repeated. Mary says it's from the Akashic Records, which you're not supposed to look up.

Then Sunday night she and I went back up to the balcony. The Figure of Darkness was, appropriately, in a bad mood.

"Look how dead it is here," she said as soon as we got up there. I didn't say anything. It suited me fine that there wasn't anyone giving a blow job or getting fucked. I was more interested in what we'd come up there for.

But Mary went on jeering. "This Club is going down the tubes," she said as I reconsidered my positive vibrations plan.

We sat down with the ethyl and as we did it I heard the on-off sound as I stared at the dance floor. It moved back, then forth, in a perfect representation of basic positive and negative. I was starting to get a little sick but then I remembered: I was with Ethyl Mary.

"Harold," Mary called to me. She must have noticed me getting green or something.

I looked across at her from a great distance. She patted her lap and told me to put my head down. I did, and I rested a while, and I heard her giving an instruction: "Whenever you can't handle things, put your head in a different place." It sounded significant at the time.

When I felt a little better, I sat up and started the ethyl again. I thought about stopping, but I thought about how I was constantly moving, quitting jobs, generally running around from one thing to the next in my life, and I know it was the ethyl, but still, I felt, this is my life. I have to see *something* through. I mean, it was like a point of honor to handle this trip. It was the same thing that kept me at the disco until the last song was played: whatever the night put me through, I had to stand it.

I'm glad I did, because I was watching the dance floor through the dome. Don't worry, by now I was getting more casual about these things. So I was watching the dance floor through the dome and again I saw this large pulsating figure and I noticed how it slowly throbbed from side to side and connected to itself.

Enough for one trip to the balcony, I figured. I noticed that Mary had stopped doing her ethyl a while ago and she was waiting for me, so I said, "OK, can we go now?" We got up and walked kind of deliberately, which was the only way we could, down the winding iron stairs. I thought about the dance floor again and the positive and negative and the going back and forth as part of a larger movement. By connecting to itself it seemed like the resolution of the infinite question.

114

By the time we got to the bottom of the stairs I figured it out: the infinite question was the great conundrum. I turned to Mary. "So the great conundrum," I said slowly, "is part of the cycle."

"Right," she said.

Initiation Night

First Tom woke me up. "I'm so excited I can't sleep," he said. Something screeched in the background.

"What is that?" I asked, alarmed.

"Oh, that's just Baby," he explained. "Don't worry about her. She's just hungry. She can't sleep either. I am so excited about going to The Holy Spirit," he went on, "I just cannot sleep. I had to call you."

"Thanks," I said. I suggested a valium.

But it was John Jr. who presaged everything that happened that night by his call.

"What are you doing waking me up, you little queen?" I rasped into the telephone.

"Now, Harold," he whispered mysteriously and I was just about over his little boy act. I could see him there with his beanie on, holding his stuffed dog. "Harold," he said with all the pedantry of a twelve-year-old. "I have to tell you something *important.*"

"Hurry up," I said, trying not to wake up.

"Tonight is a special night," he whispered, lisping. "My roommate says it's a full moon and all the planets are in position."

"You're such a mess," I said and hung up.

John found me when I got to the disco. He was this thin little kid who was probably under age, the one Tom Sanders called Pee-Wee. However old he was, he still wasn't old enough to shave and tonight he was wearing this foreign legion hat with long flaps hanging down over his ears. He marched over to me, just about lost in his loose clothes, looking from side to side like he was in the middle of some intrigue.

"Harold," he said, "I want you to come meet my roommate. He's going to explain to you about the planets." I followed him down to the bar area in numinous silence. I figured after the way I'd acted on the phone the least I could do was meet his roommate. And anyway, I wanted to get a brief lecture on this shit.

John led me into a far corner of the bar area and we climbed three levels of banquettes. Sitting at the top was a clone. "Harold," John said, "this is Alec. Alec, Harold." Then he took off.

"Hi," I said to the Clone. I figured he was maybe in his early thirties, like most of them. He had blondish-red short hair and a moustache. I remembered that John had told me his roommate had once studied Buddhism in Tibet, or Oxford, or somewhere. He claimed to know what he was talking about, is what I mean.

"I understand you want to know more about this place," he said.

"Yes," I said, figuring John had told him some of the things we'd been discussing about the Club. I thought I might learn a few things. "I'd be quite interested in anything you could tell me," I said politely.

I let him get away with looking at me with a tolerant, sage amusement. "Here," he said. "Let's do some very good cocaine first." He spooned it out for us.

117

"Let's start with the physical structure of the place," he said. "Notice," he lectured, "that everything is constructed in threes. There are three rooms of entrance, as in the old temples: one where you are first admitted and your credentials checked, the lobby. One where you pay your money as all worshippers make some sort of payment as obeisance. And one where only the faithful are admitted.

"Then," he went on, "the Club itself has three levels: the bar area on the first level, the dance floor on the second, and the balcony on the third. And there are three ways to ascend to the other levels: the marble stairs in the front of the Club, the winding, black iron stairs in the bar area that lead right up to the balcony (a quick and fleeting means to the highest level), and the rectangular-planed, black iron stairs in back of this area (a slower, yet nonetheless as sure, means upward).

"Notice too," he said, and we did more cocaine, "that everything is constructed to flow outward from a center. This floor flows in an outward spiral from the bar, to the outer levels of banquettes, totalling three, and the banquettes themselves have three levels. The dance floor works outward from the tree in the center with the star machine above it.

"And think about the structure of the music, and the intensity of the energy we put into it. The d.j. leads the ritual as the singular high priest of the function. And when we add drugs to that, and some of the instruments that some of the dancers play, we have all the elements of a religion," he said plainly. Then my drugs started to kick in as I was thinking about this and I really started to trip. I was hearing the ethyl sound.

118

"Why don't we go up to the dance floor," the Clone suggested and, as an acolyte, all I could do was obediently agree. He led me up to a far side where I never danced before, a whole other side where I figured there were probably people who came to the Club as often as I did who I didn't even know. He walked me into the middle and he said, looking at the mirrored base of the tree, "See how in the very center we confront ourselves." I could see exactly what he meant. I was amazed by the grand unfolding of it all.

The Clone started playing his fingerbells and I started dancing, and in the darkness of the dance floor I saw rectangles of light forming around me. I was dancing in the middle of energy fields. Some other clone danced by who Alec knew. "This is Rudy," Alec said. "He also knows." And Rudy nodded and smiled and danced by the side of the energy field and then moved on. Someone else I recognized danced by and did the same thing. I thought maybe they all belonged there. It was like the scene in *The Wizard of Oz* where it's the tornado and Dorothy's in the house while it's flying around and she's watching all the people she knows sail by her window, acting out. Another guy I knew danced by and nodded to me. Another guy I'd shared a house with one summer danced through and said, "Hello, Harold," and I thought they all knew about this stuff already and they were part of this ceremony arranged tonight, and I was being let in on it.

Then I looked to the side of me and I see this huge copper triangle, a pyramid, that revealed itself on the dance floor. Then everybody formed together in a gleaming mass of lights that started to fall weightlessly through the darkness and it felt like being in love, and that's when the Clone called me back.

He led me over to the banquettes on the side of the dance floor. "This is a special night," he said. "It only happens once every year, when the sun and all the planets in our solar system are aligned and everyone comes together for the ceremony of bringing in one more person. This is your initiation."

I was still tripping my brains out. "How did you know to tell me all this?" I whispered deeply.

"Because," he explained clearly and patiently, "I could see that you knew, and you were alone in your knowledge."

"How will I know," I asked him, dead serious, "that I will be able to do this for someone else?"

"The role of the master," he said solemnly, "is to serve. Now," he concluded, "we can bring your experience to its peak. Now we can go to my apartment where I will fist fuck you. Then, you will fist fuck me. And from now on, you will dance on this side of the dance floor among the other fist fuckers."

"I don't think this is the right time for me to do something like that," I said. Suddenly I wanted to know where the fuck John was during all this. "I have to find John Jr.," I said responsibly.

The Clone smiled curtly, and nodded.

A new drug

On Monday I was walking to work, really pleased about everything I learned and remembered this weekend. I was definitely worn out, and maybe a little glad it was over.

I thought about things I'd heard during the week. Someone sent a letter complaining about Joannie's hair. He said she hit him in the face with it when she danced, but I was prepared to write in her defense. Not only was Joannie's hair absolutely immobile, the sight of her four feet of straight black hair suddenly wafting above the crowd on the dance floor about seven in the morning always meant two things, that she'd finally gotten there and that it must be Sleaze.

Then I was complaining to Robert that it seems like we've been doing the same drugs forever, and when are they going to come up with something new and then Robert displayed his talent for announcing a new source of pleasure, this time the new drug.

It seemed like everybody heard of it all at once because suddenly there it was and people were talking about special K. Everything was K. Tom Sanders showed up with a box of Special K and posed with it. He walked around from spot to spot. There were Special K T-shirts.

"Ah love K," Tom said and stood there holding the box. "The undisputed drug of homosexuals everywhere," he delivered.

Robert turned me on to it for the first time at the top of the black iron stairs. "Here," he said. "Let's do some K," and I caught a flash of this enormous triangular lever, and I wondered where the hell did he get such a spectacular coke implement, at Tiffany's? A corner of it went up my nose. The last thing I heard him say was "Bye-bye," from far away and he disappeared.

I followed him up the stairs while I waited for the drug to kick in. Listen, if you try this drug you'll probably want it every week. You might want to live on it. I was on the dance floor and within a couple of minutes everything around me darkened and then paled. It started looking portentous. People turned white, getting completely opaque and moving very slowly, as if the movements were broken down in time. It was like it was programmed. Everyone was there who was supposed to be there, and they were all doing what they were supposed to be doing.

When that wore off, after an hour or so, I had to have more. This time we were sitting on the grey cubes behind the steps to the dance floor. I watched everything get cloudy. I looked at Robert and his profile was huge and two dimensional, like we were on the inside of the TV. I couldn't believe we were really doing this.

"Robert," I asked him, "what are we doing?"

The image of his head rotated and looked at me. "I just remembered that question again," he said. "The one I can never remember the answer to. You know," he went on, "how you know that space and time are like, infinite. And you believe it even though you can't possibly understand it."

"Well, I can remember the *answer*," I interrupted, "I just can never remember the *ques-*

122

tion." Speech was getting more difficult. "If the question is how can space and time be infinite? the answer is The Great Conundrum. You know, that back-and-forth thing we always just understand here."

"That's this place for you," he said standing up. "It has amazing revelations and healing powers."

He must be a mess, I thought as I followed him up the dance floor, otherwise he'd never admit that about The Holy Spirit. I was a mess too; there was a staircase leading up and off to somewhere and people were passing through it. The contingents, with their bodies whitened, were formally entering and exiting. This was something going on in the subtext. The dance floor looked completely different and it was still familiar. Here's how it was: like a special place we've never been to and have always known.

My legs lifted without feeling. John bounded up to the dance floor, and then Himiko appeared and she nodded to me. It was probably nine in the morning and I hadn't seen her before then. I wondered what was going on with her.

I headed down the stairs with no particular direction and who did I run into but Ethyl Mary. We were facing each other in opposite directions on the staircase, each clutching the handrail. "Mary, what is going on here?" I asked, like something was going on and she would know what it was.

And she answered me just as seriously, more, and she said (and now I wonder what she was on, because if I was that fucked up, she must have been too, to be talking to me), "Do you want to talk about it?" in this very clipped, tense way which I guess we were, considering all that speed.

So do you have this?

Me, deep and fast: Mary, just what is going *on* here?

Her, tensely, like it's possible to discuss: Do you want to talk about it?

Me, like this is making any sense at all: Yes (intently).

We walked quickly into the bar area and we climbed up on one of the banquettes and Mary said to me, didactically, "It's very evil." She lit a cigarette, puckering it in her lips, flipped the match, tossed it in an ashtray.

"No," I said, convinced we had to make it good.

"It is," she said, crossing her arms.

"Mary," I said, "it can be good or it can be evil," I told her, since I figured we both knew she was causing it. We had to make it good, I finally realized. We could resolve any duality by force of mind; just by deciding something we could make it so. I thought of Native American theology: that words have power. And in that minute, I felt that Tom Sanders was not there to destroy me, he was there for something good. And the world wasn't going to blow up from The Dance Club. With a force of mind, we could make something fabulous happen from there.

She said, "Well, do you hear it breathing?"

Did I hear it *breathing?*

Actually, I did, but I didn't want to dwell on *that* so I said to her, and by now it was a real physical effort to speak, I said one word at a time, "It can be good."

Are you imagining me trying to talk, K'd out of my mind? It was coming out like 16 revolutions per minute, I'm sure, like an accident victim learning to speak again. And I was trying to convince Ethyl Mary of all people not to be negative.

"No," she answered. "It can't." I stood up and I saw Mexico City, brown and dusty buildings, crumble and fall to the ground.

Then I wasn't even recovered from this incident, I was walking around and I saw Santos, and he read me in moments, before I even saw it coming. "Why, darling," he said. "What a lovely T-shirt," or something like that. Who could converse?

"Thanks," I forced speech. "I never pay much attention to these things. I got half my clothes out of unclaimed baggage from JFK."

"That's you, honey," he said. "Isn't it? Unclaimed Baggage." Then he said, "Excuse me, I have to go talk to some people," or something like that and he was gone.

Art

"So what are you going to do about the Club?" I asked Mary the next Saturday night. We were sitting up in the grey stairs. "If you really think something's going wrong for you?"

"I don't know," she said, exasperated. "This seems to be a pattern. I went through four husbands the way I've gone through this disco."

"Four husbands?" I asked. "Nobody goes through four marriages anymore."

"I have," she said. "I met my first husband at UCLA, while I was finishing up my bachelor's in political science. That marriage lasted two years, until around the time my first travel agency became really successful. He didn't like the diversion of my time."

"What'd you call your agency?" I asked. "Ethyl Trips?"

"No," she said. "Acme. My second husband died. My third husband I divorced after a month. He was a wash-out. My fourth husband now works for the CIA. You can imagine why he and I didn't get along.

"I sold the two travel agencies six or seven years ago, when I was thirty-two, with an agreement that I'd stay out of the business. That was fine, because by then I wanted to open a nightclub, so I opened up Hell on Wheels on Fourteenth Street. I'd had practice from the coffeehouse I ran in the Village in the late Sixties. Then

I dropped the management of Hell on Wheels because I decided I'd rather be a customer than the manager. That was when my third husband and I split up."

"He wasn't into S&M?" I asked.

"No," she said. "Though I did try to interest him."

"What about the other stuff?" I asked.

"De nada," she said. "Zip."

"When are you going to get married again?" I asked her.

"Never. Four times is enough. And who's going to want a wife who spends her days comatose and her nights in a disco? Thank you, no, I'd rather be in the disco. And besides, who would I get for bridesmaids at this point, the Hells Angels?"

"Aren't they your friends?"

"That's not the point," she said.

"Do you want to go down and dance?" I asked her.

"I want to stay up here and think awhile," she said. "I just want to look at the dome. You go on down."

I found Santos at twelve o'clock. He was wearing a leather tunic, some kind of loose animal hide pulled in at his waist, and his hair was completely shaved on the sides. There was one multi-colored streak running down the middle.

"Do you love the look?" he asked from behind his sunglasses. "This is Urban Warrior."

"I do love it, Santos," I said. "It's just too you."

"Isn't it, though?" he asked. "Thank you, baby." Then he looked around him. "Let's get away from these trash," he said. "Would you like some coke?"

We sat down on a banquette and he pulled out this leather pouch and in it was a plastic bag that probably had an ounce of cocaine in it. We did some and then we went onto the dance floor.

Then he started a commentary. "It is very important," he began, his mouth moved tensely below the mirrored glasses, "to know that we are artists. We are beyond stars; anyone can be a star, it's business. Remember that, baby. We are artists." He took off his glasses and handed me his tambourine. "Feel its power," he said. "This is the artist's expression. And you know what? There's room for you in this."

A clone stepped out of a group of men and stood in front of us. He stared at Santos and his fists clenched. Santos stared back. Playing regally, he held up his tambourine. The clone tensed. I'd never seen hostility on the dance floor before; I was afraid he was going to beat the shit out of us.

Their eyes were streaming into each other, and then it broke; the guy's eyes softened. His body relaxed, he moved back into his group. Santos played like nothing had happened but the light streaming in his eyes thickened and brightened. Somebody leaned over and whispered, "Honey, you better put your sunglasses back on."

Santos turned to me. "Law and order," he declared. His head cocked and his expression was unwavering. "It's the *Law* of the *Land.*"

I blinked. I wondered just how many people there knew about these Natural Order things.

128

Later I was downstairs; I was sitting on top of a banquette listening to a heavy and labored breathing. I looked around since it was pretty late, and I didn't see anyone in the next banquette. Then I looked up and I saw the air vent. Then I remembered a discussion Mary and I had one night when she asked me if I could hear someone breathing.

I looked up at the air vent again. Mary's monster.

The White Party

Tickets for the White Party were advance sales only, two guests to a member. For the month before, the men's shops on Christopher Street displayed white jeans, white shorts, Tommy Tailor tank tops and anything else that'd move. But that was only Christopher Street. On the Lower East Side, where David Walken and I lived and shopped, you had to look a bit harder, but you could find white uniforms, pajamas and riding pants.

At the event: floor to ceiling white mylar covered the walls, hanging in sheets. White venetian blinds suspended from the ceiling to the tops of the banquettes in the living room. To walk around, you had to negotiate a forest of white branches and tiny lights.

This was the most crowded I'd seen the Club. As I stood on the back stairs, halfway up and halfway down, the downstairs area was a living mass of white cloaked people, moving and surging, propelled by drugs and restricted by density: it was a Ziegfeld production, and the crowd from an aerial view was an undulating white feathered wing, beginning to flap almost imperceptibly under the microscope of the eye in the sky.

I walked the rest of the way up; going back down to the living room would have been impossible. At the top landing before twelve o'clock there was hardly any room either, but there was some. Shirtless boys with handsome hair on developing chests were dancing there since there was no room on the dance floor.

I looked back down at the stairs: a long haired queen in a wedding gown was walking up. She was a paraplegic and the arms of the gown were sewn across her chest like a straitjacket. She passed me and entered the dance floor.

I followed her in, just to look because there was no room. But I had to work in as a Diana Ross song came on and I was moving and acting out with the crowd. As she triumphantly declared she wasn't going to cry no more or spend no more sleepless nights I cried into my T-shirt, acting out each part and working my way in deeper. The tree rose out of the center of the floor and as it rose to full height and expanse over the dancers, black-lighted arms of the tree reverberated as the room went dark and our white outfits were electrified. "It's a nice day for a/white wedding," Billy Idol promised us as it peaked.

The dance floor started to fill with more people than the dancers; there were others standing around as well, and the banquettes were crowded with people standing facing a temporary stage at seven o'clock. The music stopped on a downbeat and a voice came up.

"Gentlemen," it said, "The Holy Spirit is pleased to present Miss Jolene Jomama." The dancers cheered, clapping their hands over their heads as the opening beats of her hit came up and part of the dome wall at seven o'clock disengaged, rising to reveal the diva standing there with her mike. Her head was bowed.

"Thank you," she said loudly, shaking her hair, looking around at the crowd. "Thank you," she repeated as the intro beats brought her into the beginning of her hit.

She walked back and forth the breadth of the elevated stage as she sang her song and with each high point the crowd's cheering rose as they applauded her. She was smiling, she was sweating and she was tossing her hair. I doubted she'd ever had such audience appreciation.

She was strutting and singing quickly on the upbeats as the lights spotted her and worked the room, orange, blue, then purple. I walked the perimeter of the dance floor, moving carefully around the people clustered at the banquettes. The lights flashed and revealed a face catching my eye at the same moment; then the light changed and the figure was gone as I was still moving around the circumference.

I slipped out the nine o'clock entrance, moving through the crowd gathered there below the dance floor, and found a spot outside the dome, behind where the stage had been constructed for the night. There was a crowd here too, packed adoring men worshiping the performing diva and as they watched up at the back of the stage, I looked behind them at the back wall of the second floor. The diva's shadow was gyrating wildly as the real woman sang, the dark image moving and shaking like the shadow of a jungle princess working it before the fire in the cave.

I looked up at the back of the stage and she was into her second song. Slipping through this behind-the-stage crowd I made my way back up and around, entering the dance floor at six o'clock. I found Tom Sanders and David Walken.

"Harold," David said, wired from MDA. Tom was dancing sideways, transfixed by the diva.

Then the orange lights flashed again, the room going dark precisely on Jolene Jomama's downbeat; then immediately they came back up on her upbeat but the room was white now, and yellow. "David," I said, "look: now this is a different place. We're in this gymnasium in a middle American town we grew up in."

"And they've allocated this space for us," he said. Then the lights changed again back to the blue and purple that Jolene started on as she finished her song. The cheering rose, peaking; Tom applauded heavily as I clapped with my hands over my head. David sat back against a banquette as the scene returned to normal; Jolene lowered her head as the piece of the dome lowered back into place; the lights darkened again and the planetarium projection on the ceiling of the dome meant we were back under the night sky again.

The queen with no arms passed by again. She'd shed her wedding gown and was by now walking around in white bikini briefs. I looked at David; Tom danced into the crowd, his arms raised upward like he was shooting baskets, his eyes closed reverently. Michael, the Michael from the gym who'd given Lenny a hard time, came up to us.

"Hi, guys," he said. He wore loose white shorts, white E. G. Smith socks and tank top.

"Michael," David said, wide-eyed.

"Michael," I said, "doesn't it feel like the Universe has been through a lot tonight?"

"Yeah," he said flatly. "Right."

Then he winked. "I'm so embarrassed," he said. "I arranged for Susan to come tonight. Did you see what she's wearing?"

"White toreadors and a candy cane jacket," David said.

"I think she looks pretty," I said.

"So do I," Michael said. "That's not why I'm embarrassed. I feel bad for her. The manager sent one of his minions over to tell her to tone it down next time or she'll be asked to leave. I think it was her hair that did it."

"She is very pretty," I said. "And her hair is no longer than the Queen with No Arms."

"Did you see her?" Michael asked.

"How could we not?" David said. "Not only didn't she have any arms, she was wearing a wedding gown."

"Work it, I say," Michael said.

"Can you believe how fabulous this party is?" David asked.

"I sure can," Michael said.

"I feel like we're in a computer," David said, watching yellow portal spots lighting synchronously up the expanse of the dome, but far from the disco ball. "I just mean," he said in his earnest way, "It's like everything here is happening in a programmed mode. On a computer printout."

"That's your K, darling," Michael said. "Hello, Diana," he said, his head tilting just a little.

"Hello, Michael," she kissed him. She was wearing a white hooded Kamali. She and David hugged. "It's nice to see you again, Harold," she told me. "Would you boys care to join me in some ethyl?" she asked.

"How lovely," we said. We sat down on the banquette as Diana held the bottle in her lap.

"I just remembered something," she said as her brown eyes looked at each of us.

"You don't have a rag," Michael said.

"I have one in my locker," I offered. "It belongs to *Ethyl Mary.*"

"I'd rather die," Diana said. "Michael," she realized, "you have another shirt in your locker, don't you?"

"Wait," David said. He said a few words to someone next to us, then handed Diana a clean, folded rag.

"David," Diana said simply. We did the ethyl, looked at the dome, tripped.

"Let's do some K," Michael suggested. He spooned some out for each of us. He was about to offer some to David's acquaintance, the man who'd loaned us the rag.

The slim, moustached man stopped him politely. "Who'd you get it from?" he asked, his eyes somber above his moustache.

Michael told him.

The man made a quick, impatient gesture, stood up, and took a vial from his pocket. "Please have some of this," he said, spooning some out for each of us. "Now isn't that good K?" he asked when we were done.

"It certainly is," we agreed. He smiled and left.

"Excuse me," Diana said, standing. "I have to go make a phone call."

David, Michael and I watched her leave. "It must be seven in the morning in the middle of the White Party," Michael said. "And Diana has to go make a phone call?"

I was still confused. "What was that all about with that man?" I asked David.

"I have no idea," he said, shaking his head.

"Do you?" I asked Michael.

"No," he said.

"Did you even know him?" I asked David. David shook his head, unconcerned. "Let's go downstairs," I suggested. "Let's look for Tom Sanders."

Tom was in the living room watching the video. A NASA rocket was taking off.

"Golly, that's something, isn't it?" he was saying to a man next to him.

"It sure is," the man said. In a polo shirt and his hair thinning, he looked like an accountant or a member of the middle class; perhaps he was passing through here on his way to somewhere else. "Can you believe the tragedy this week about that NASA rocket exploding?"

"It was awful," Michael said, sitting down next to them.

"Oh, please," I said. "What a lot of opportunistic jingo-ism."

"What is he talking about?" the accountant asked Tom, his face furrowing.

"Nothing," Tom said.

"I thought it was so sad on television when I was watching the President consoling the families," Michael continued. "They showed him going up to each one of them."

"I just want to know what he *said* to all of them," David said.

The accountant's mind went to something else. "Have you danced yet?" he asked.

"No," Michael said for us. "It's much too early. We're waiting for Sleaze."

We laughed; and walked around to hang out somewhere else a while before we could dance, before the dance floor would empty out a bit. As it happened that night, it wasn't danceable until noon, and we danced for five hours after that.

136

At the end of the evening there were still two thousand people in the place. But we knew the end was coming: around three-thirty the d.j. broke for applause which we happily gave him. Robbie was a master. At four he did it again, in the last hour.

When he broke at five we knew it was the end and we cheered him; some dancers stomped their feet. Then he brought up Sam Harris' version of "Over The Rainbow" for the last song and the light show. We sat around the compass of the banquettes and watched the light man create a visual symphony. This was the secret of the closing light show, and only the dancers who stayed till the end every week knew about it.

Then we climbed down the stairs to the first level, got our things from our lockers or from coatcheck, and walked out the black riveted-steel, mail-like doors. Mercifully, it was raining.

The next day there was a story in the *Daily News* about a jumper on the roof of the Club building; evidently there was a guest at the White Party who couldn't handle the party or special K. He said he was trying to escape from hell and there were devils inside. The article didn't mention the Club name.

Tom Sanders dances alone among strangers

Around this time things started to change and Mary wasn't the only one who felt something missing in her relationship with the Club. Attendance was down somewhat and some people who I saw there every weekend started to miss a Saturday here and there. Himiko wasn't there.

And I found Tom Sanders dancing alone, in the middle of strangers. I liked him better now that I'd decided that everything in the Club was good, so it couldn't be that he was there to destroy the very essence of my being. "What are you doing here?" I asked him.

"What do you mean?" he asked me as he opened his eyes solemnly and continued his up-and-down dancing.

"Stop that," I said to him. "Where'd you learn to dance like that?"

"What's going on?" he asked, opening his eyes wider.

"I don't know," I said. "I come over here, really by accident to a completely foreign part of the dance floor, and I find you dancing right in the middle of all this. Now what are you doing over here?"

He sighed. "It's about Robert," he said winsomely.

"Oh," I said. "I know. Did you see his new boyfriend?"

"Yes," he said. "Of course I saw him."

138

"That means," I said, "that when you weren't looking, Robert took a new boyfriend, a position you'd now be holding if you'd been a little more attentive."

"I know," he said. "I don't know which was worse, his last boyfriend or his taking up with this little blond."

"Yeah. I know," I said. "Don't you hate little blonds? Well, listen," I said. "There's something I never told you about Robert. I mean, I didn't think you were going to carry this so far."

"What do you mean?" he asked.

"Well," I said, "have you ever noticed the way he dances?"

"Course I have," Tom said.

"Have you ever noticed," I went on, "that in the dance of the pursuer and the pursued—you know the one Robert calls the Walk; the one I call the Spirit in Search of Itself— Robert is always the pursued?"

"You're right," Tom said.

"Well, if he's the pursued, what does that tell us about his probable sexual preferences, vis a vis your own?"

Tom looked at me out of the sides of his black eyes. "You're telling me I've been wasting my time," he said.

"I'm telling you, honey," I said, "that it's time to go back to your own side of the dance floor." I touched his sleeve. "Come on."

History

I ran up the stairs in my Calvin Klein jockey shorts and size ten pumps. My feet were already swelling even though I had just started getting dressed.

Although it was early in the summer season there was only a little time left before the social season at The Holy Spirit closed. I ran back down the stairs of the house we'd rented. All I'd wanted to do was run up and down a moment that way. I went back to my room and pulled on the tight navy skirt I found downtown and the silk polka dot blouse I had to go with it. It stretched across my pecs tightly so I stuck out my chest. I figured I could do without accoutrement there. I'm not overdeveloped, but the tight trim bodice was attractive, I thought. I clipped on my earrings, checked my makeup again, and went back up-stairs.

Bobby, dressed in a pink pinafore with a long brown wig and pearls, looked like a garish parody of a sixteen-year-old. But what do I know about Long Island Jewish girls, I thought. For all I know that's exactly what they look like. "Honey," I stopped myself from telling Bobby he looked like a whore. "You look lovely."

"Thank you, darling," Bobby said pertly, clearly pleased. He loped from right to left just like he did with his shirt off, running around the disco. "So do you," he remembered to add.

"My dear," Charles, a freckled older man, smacked his lips coming across the room. "You look like somebody's mother." He held his hand to his forehead and looked like he was about to swoon from all the gin he'd consumed. On short notice he'd scrounged up a nightgown and a brown wig, and with his eyes shut and his gin glass in place, he did look like a suburban middle class alcoholic, if that was the intention.

"Well, yes, I look like somebody's mother," I bothered to tell him. "I look like my own," I explained, admiring my own trim figure and my choice of a classic outfit, pancake and red lipstick. I'd pursed my lips on a kleenex just like my mother does.

Anthony, the receptionist from the gym, came up the stairs looking like Shirley MacLaine in a black pant suit and heavy rouge and a red wig. Derek, who was black and even bigger and more muscular than Anthony, followed him in a towel wrapped around his torso and another wrapped around his head. Another queen who'd forgotten her outfit; at least he looked chastised.

Franklin and Paul made up for it. Franklin, who had said "Oh, I couldn't," when I called during the week and suggested a drag dinner for Memorial Day, had quickly overcome his obstacle and "dug up" a showgirl's g-string shimmer outfit and headdress. Petite and muscular, his strong legs carried him perfectly in the matching open heels. "Why, that looks wonderful on you," I exclaimed. "Like it was hanging in your closet waiting for you."

"Thank you," Franklin said, trying not to preen too obviously since it would have been below his social, or at least his economic, station.

"I asked Halston to whip it up for me," he said. "If you can't rely on your close friends, who can you rely on?" He looked around for an answer and caught my eye.

Does he actually expect me to commiserate? I wondered. Instead I said, "I know what you mean. I try to rely on Halston as often as I can." I congratulated myself on my subtlety. Franklin's face went from sincerely quizzical to slightly nasty very quickly.

Paul, his boyfriend and companion that summer, towered over him with a tall and svelte frame. He wore a black wool cocktail dress and a blond wig. "I need a drink," he said insipidly.

The phone rang. "It's probably *Andy,*" Paul said, referring to Franklin's employer, to whom Franklin had referred perhaps once or twice already. In fact it was for him, and he took the call. I actually respected Franklin as someone who had gone through one full era and had not only visibly survived, he was living successfully in this one. We should all take a lesson, I thought. Franklin had even taken heroin.

Greg and David came upstairs looking like two Italian whores. I suspected they were already K'd out from the careful way they walked, even in flats. I couldn't believe they were wearing flats when, with their sizes six or seven, they could have found fabulous spikes. I suffered while David took it easy. It almost pissed me off.

We sat down to dinner and I immediately got up and ran downstairs. I wanted them all to see me hurry in heels two sizes too small. "Wait," I said. "I almost forgot something," and hurried back upstairs with a small package. I stood at the head of the table.

"I have a presentation to make," I said. "To the youngest member of our house. For her first summer on Fire Island," and I presented the book to Paul. Paul unwrapped it and exclaimed limply over the Strand copy of *Dancer from the Dance*. "It's a little yellow, but it's out of print," I said. "And this is a first edition."

We sat around the gloomy poolhouse that was Anthony's bedroom that summer. Our heels were kicked off and in a pile. The rain came down in light drips on the glass doors as we passed around the opium bong. Things were bleak and not intriguing.

"I don't know," David said. I looked at him. His frosted wig was still in place, but his lipstick was smeared from dinner, and his silk blouse was opened.

"I just don't feel like we're all *doomed*," he said.

Primitivism...

Somewhere in the Club Tom Sanders was clapping bawdily at some outrage while Brian Owen's laugh rose and fell, hyena-like, around the whole lower level. I walked up to the dance floor and stood near nine o'clock. Himiko tapped me on the shoulder. "Hey, Harold," she said, "we haven't danced together."

"I haven't been dancing a lot lately." I was kind of embarrassed to admit it.

"You too?" she answered. Himiko not dancing? This was the woman I saw on my first night there that season, someone who personified the Dance to me. "I know how it is," she went on. "I haven't been having a good time at all either. I get a little worked about the drugs, sometimes, too."

"You're kidding," I said. "You shouldn't get worked about the drugs. Drugs're good for you. I would've killed myself a long time ago if it weren't for drugs. They made me understand things I never would've seen otherwise."

"What kinds of things?" she asked, holding my eyes steadily.

"About how it works here, what's really going on."

She looked at me, then away. Then, in the darkness, she motioned me downward with her hand, down the seven steps to the banquettes below.

...explained

"What kinds of things?" she asked me again, sitting in the darkness against the banquette. I looked directly in her eyes. Her hair was short, with bangs and a cowlick, and she wore a long sleeve T-shirt with jeans, torn at the knee.

"Well, when I first started coming here in September, I didn't have any beliefs," I started. She just watched me. Her eyes darted over to the lights streaming from the dance floor and then came back to me.

"I mean," I said, "I wasn't an atheist or anything. And I wasn't an agnostic. I just didn't believe anything. But coming here and dancing, I started to see some things and I started to understand a few things. And at first I thought everyone here knew about them."

"Most people don't," she said.

"That took me a while to figure out," I said. "I thought everyone here saw the same things I did. That we were creating energy here and it was building up, like really big, under the dome. I mean, everyone looked like they all knew the same thing... that what was happening here was parallel to the world. The energy built up so strong that every Saturday I thought something was going to happen but I couldn't figure out what it was. For a while I thought the world was going to blow up and I figured maybe the President was going to push the missile launch button at the same moment we built the energy up to its highest point."

"That's pretty drastic," she said.

"This is a drastic place," I said. A few late dancers wandered past us. I watched two people sit down on the other banquette to take drugs and look up at the lights. "But then I realized, whatever was going to happen could be something very good instead. I realized we could direct the energy into something positive. We could control it with our minds. Then I stopped thinking the world was going to end. I mean, the moment of all that tension just passed politically. It could still happen, I guess, but I just don't feel it will. The point is, I saw us creating energy by our dancing and I learned we could control things with our minds.

"I never believed in reincarnation before I came here," I went on, "but now I do. Because I saw that when we release energy, it has to go somewhere. Something has to happen to it...I figure that's how lifeforms must catch on. Energy gets released and it has to catch and gestate. So like when someone dies, the energy probably shoots out in some direction as their body falls away. It has to go somewhere, since it shoots out so fast." I hesitated. I was talking a lot for my first real conversation with her.

"Do you believe in God?" she asked me. She sat back and put her arm over her knee.

"I believe in the Energy Collective," I said. "And I know you do too. That's why I've been wanting to discuss this stuff with you, because a lot of it I figured out when I was on the dance floor with you. A lot of it came to me in pure thoughts, and I knew that sometimes I was reading your

146

mind, and sometimes I was getting thoughts from other people who know about this stuff too.

"And other times I was probably just being given knowledge directly. No, not being given knowledge," I corrected myself. "I was in a state where there weren't any obstructions to my remembering things the basic me knows."

"That's the part of you that's the essence of your being," she smiled. "The Harold-ness behind your present lifeform," she said. "Do you follow?"

"Yeah," I said. "Sure." The lights streamed around us. Colors were reverberating against the dome.

"When I dance I feel my vibrational level increasing," she said. "I've felt my mind getting very open and I get a lot of thoughts from other people. Sometimes it's hard." She smiled again. "That's why I stopped coming for a while."

"I don't understand," I said.

"You think about God when you dance," she said. "Or the Energy Collective. But not everyone does. A lot of people come here to look for sex."

"You're kidding," I said, shocked. I mean, I came there to dance.

"No," she said. "Remember that this is a disco and a lot of the energy you see here is sexual energy. That's what a lot of people go out for. They come here and take drugs. A lot of them see things like you, but they can't believe them and anyway they're looking for other things. But you're very lucky, Harold," she said.

"Yeah," I said. "I know."

She stood up off the banquette and wiped her palms against her jeans. "Let's dance," she said.

Ethyl Mary splits

I asked Mary about it. "Mary," I said, "do you believe that some people just come here for sex?"

"Of course I do," she said. "That's why nine-tenths of the people come here."

"Sex," I said. "Yuk. Who would want to have sex?"

"You're weird," she said. "Hey guys," she turned to some clones sitting around her.

"Don't tell them," I panicked. I mean, it's not the kind of thing you want getting around. "Listen," I said. "Let me ask you another question. Do you think the world is going to end soon?"

"No."

"Why not?" I asked. "I mean, given the fact that for the first time in history, we have the means to blow up the planet. And not only that, but two opposing forces are manifested in two geographically massive superpowers."

"No," she said inexpressively. "I don't believe the world is getting ready to blow up. I'll say that we've come closer than we've come before. But this happens cyclically. And the fact that you think about these things at all just shows the potential of this Club. So many more people could have understood what you do here, and yet the Club's on a decline.

"I hate the management of this place. I'd love to eviscerate the manager. I'd love to disembowel him. I'd love to slit open his stomach with a kitchen knife and personally remove his intestines."

"What would you think about blowing the place up?" I asked her. "If The Holy Spirit closed, something else could open."

"You can't do that," she said and launched into an oratory. I realized I should have started from the opposite premise. "A," she began, "it's someone else's property. B, people could get hurt. And C, some people still like the place."

"Mary," I said, "I'm sure you, of all people, believe in action."

"I do," she said. "Here's what I suggest. Don't blow up the Club. Blow up the locker room. And do it after hours. This way probably no one will get hurt, and the damage will be enough to close the place, but not to hurt it.

"And don't use TNT," she continued. "Use plastique. Now, where were you planning to get these explosives?"

"I was sort of hoping you might know."

"Who do you think I am," she said, "the Weather Underground?"

"Well, yes," I said. "I did kind of suspect."

"Just for the record," she said, "be sure never to ask me that on the phone. It's bugged. And you know me well enough to know I'd never be part of some ship of fools that blows up its own headquarters. Find some plastique," she said. "That's your challenge."

"And what are you going to do?" I asked.

"Me? I've had it," she said. "I've had it with this Club. It's over. It's dead. There're two new clubs opening next month, and I heard about another one opening uptown. I'm leaving."

She stood there in her cloth coat, looking at me. She held her black pocketbook with its gold colored snap.

"Well, goodbye," I said. I kissed her.

"Goodnight," she said. "Don't do anyone I wouldn't do. And call me. Now go inside. I don't want you to watch me leave."

"Mary's leaving," I told Tom.

"Aw, I don't believe that," he said.

"It's true." I was confused. Mary actually left. But she'd been unhappy there, and for all the time I was there and having a fabulous time, all she could talk about were the good old days. I resolved never to live in the past. "Now what?" I asked Tom.

"Now wait and see what happens," he said.

I wanted to change the subject. "Now tell me more about Bobby's new boyfriend," I said.

"Oh, I actually met him," Tom said. "We were going into the Black Rock Cafe on Sixth Avenue for lunch on Saturday and there was Bobby and his new boyfriend."

"How's the guy?" I asked. "What's he like?"

"*Very* attractive," Tom said. "Very handsome in a wasp sort of way."

"You mean 'that' wasp sort of way, don't you?" I asked. "There's only one way, so far as I've been able to notice, and they all look the same. Like Saks ads."

"That's it exactly," Tom said. "He was even more handsome than the guys in the Saks ads."

"And he was a wasp. Did he recognize you as a wasp too? Was he embarrassed to be dating a Jewish person in the presence of another wasp?"

"Oh, no," Tom said. "I was dressed up in my Fourteenth Street clothes and was wearing my painter's cap and I hadn't shaved for at least a day or two."

"So in other words, he recognized you as a fellow and gazed at you as if to say, 'You are a disgrace.'"

"Right," Tom said. "I'm a disgrace."

"You're a *disgrace.*" I started to get exuberant. "Isn't it fabulous?"

"I love it," Tom said intensely. "I love being a disgrace."

The liquor bar

But Tom and I felt different about things the next day; maybe we were crashing. He picked me up on Second Avenue and Tenth Street, in front of St. Mark's-in-the-Bowery. He was gripping the steering wheel and there was a cigarette hanging out of his mouth about as carelessly as it could look and he hadn't shaved either. Which I don't mean to imply that he was less presentable than usual though he certainly looked his part.

"Wahl, get in," he insisted, releasing the door.

"What's eating you?" I asked.

"What's eating me," he explained edgily, "is that I just spent all of last night doing an eighth of cocaine with Brian Owen." He stepped on the accelerator and jumped the light. "Get out of the way," he screamed hoarsely out the window. "Fuckin' idiots."

We both laughed. He toured through the early morning Second Avenue traffic, a couple of buses, a few cars and a cab, also the delivery trucks for the egg market, the chicken house, and such places.

"Girl," he said, "I hope you're still laughin' when I tell you what Brian Owen told me." Brian worked in the office at The Holy Spirit.

I lit a joint and handed it to Tom and he sucked on it ferociously. "Wahl," he said, "it seems that due to declining revenues, our private Club is opening to the public."

I banged the dashboard with my fist and Tom slammed on the brake. We stopped short before a red light across the street from the Club. I looked at the bare grey entrance, the one we slipped into quietly every weekend. "Take a good look," Tom said. "Because your fabulous entrance is being closed."

"The liquor bar?" I asked.

"That's right," he said. "To get their liquor license they had to use the side street address. They couldn't get one for the main address because of the Greek Church across the street. So no more fabulous entrance. They're constructing one on the emergency exit."

"Liquor," I said. "I knew liquor would ruin the Club. How can we have people coming there and *drinking?* They have to take drugs."

"Not only that," Tom said. "Now that they have a liquor license they have to open to the public. Brian showed me invitations they printed up."

"Invitations for straight people?"

"Yeah. Like the kind you see in fern bars and health clubs and advertising agencies."

"Something is wrong," I said.

"Well, thank you, Harold Fenestere," he pronounced every syllable.

"Shut up, you nasty harbinger of things as they turn disgustingly downward," I said. "This has been coming. You must have noticed, it's not just the Club. New York's been getting boring. Look at that," I pointed out the window to a bicycle messenger carelessly pulling up to a pole on the sidewalk. "Even the bike messengers don't hustle anymore."

"You're right," Tom said despairingly.

153

"And have you been uptown lately?" I accused him and he snivelled into the steering wheel.

"No," he admitted.

"Well, don't bother," I said schizophrenogenicly. "It's boring. Remember when things were so exciting here you could see the energy flickering in the air like an old movie? Every building in this town used to look mysterious.

"And now it's a bore. Real estate's gotten too expensive so people can't afford to come here anymore. The government has let several thousand fringe people die and they're direct absentees from our social circuit and this town's core nightlife. And the music has declined to some sorry repetitious monologue that I can't believe anyone would want to dance to. And the management of The Holy Spirit has ruined the Club. The fuckers," I concluded.

"The fuckers," Tom repeated.

The beginning of the end

"Harold, wake up," Marty said on the Island. He stood over the bed, his short black hair standing up pugnaciously. Marty still had his sunglasses on and wore angular clothes over his muscular body. He looked like a high tech visitor. "We're having a morning party," he said.

I got up. "Now don't do anything," Marty said. "See how I look?" If after disco looks were acceptable to Marty they were acceptable to anyone, I figured. I followed him up the stairs to the morning room.

Michael looked up from the sofa at the coffee table. "Good morning, Harold," he said alertly. "Would you like breakfast? Some special K?"

I perched at a demure angle on the corner next to Michael as the darker, pretty boy spooned some K up my nose.

"Change the music," David said.

Someone lit a joint and it went around the table, from David to Michael to me to Marty. The music changed to more current disco and Michael started a sliding dance around the floor. I danced near him and Marty joined. David watched, a cocktail party dancer.

I opened the glass door to the terrace and sat down in the director's chair. Michael and Marty were still dancing inside.

The wind blew my hair as I looked at David, sitting across from me. I looked past his profile, over the railing of the deck, to the hazy airy view of the island. Everything was light, pale tones. David, sitting against the railing above the island, looked at me.

"We just lost thirty years," I said. "Thirty years just passed. We're going to be fifty-eight this year, instead of twenty-eight. We're in the home."

"That's K for you," David said. We were old men sitting with blankets around our legs.

"Did our careers ever take off," I asked, "or did we just keep freelancing?"

"I don't remember," David said.

"Oh," I said. "Well, I guess it doesn't matter."

"Charles is inside," David said.

I picked my head up in surprise. "Is she still here? She's still *alive?*"

"She's still alive," David said. "And she's still your roommate."

"That old reptile," I said. "It proves what I always said, that she'd live forever. Nothing would kill her. Her hide is made of mail."

"She's right inside," David continued. A breeze blew over us and I shook my hair to catch the wave

"I can't believe she's still here," I said. "That's one of the jokes of the universe in the structure of how things are, like the fact that you have sex and remove waste from the same organs. Not only is Charles still alive, she's my roommate. How did all this happen? I was growing up in Brooklyn, and then all this happened."

"It was the K," David said.

156

"Then this morning," Anthony said in the gym, his face flushing. "I'm walking down Washington Street, it's eight-thirty in the morning and what do I see but this guy's ass in the window."

"That's disgusting," Marty said. He turned to me. "This is my good workout day," he said. "I get to do anything I want." He walked over to the pull-up bar and hoisted himself up.

"Disgusting? It was an offense," Anthony persisted. "To see this sick queen's ass in the window with a dildo stuck up it was more than anyone should have to deal with at that hour. Children are awake at that hour."

"Forget children," I said. "Adults don't want to see that either."

"That's right," Anthony said. "I didn't mind when he had the levelors down and all you could see were the movies going. I didn't mind seeing those young blonds on camera. But this. First it was just his ass, with the blinds down. Then with the blinds up. And now he's got a dildo up his ass with the blinds wide open at eight-thirty in the morning. Next he's going to have the window open a crack. I can tell, we're working up to it."

"Really," I said. "If he wants to do that, he should go back to where the Anvil used to be and dig a hole."

Marty came back. "I forgot what I was doing," he said.

"Anything you want," I reminded him.

"Oh, yeah. Right," he said. "Oh, there's that queen again." He nodded subtly to the reception area, where someone we didn't like was presenting his card. "She's going to be looking for her boots," he said. His sideburns twitched.

"Wait," Anthony said. "I'll show her. And those two others, with their fucking inversion boots. They come in here and they monopolize the chin-up bar."

"And they're just so generally offensive," I added.

"I'm going to hide the boots," Anthony said. He headed over to the corner while Marty and I watched him scoop up the equipment and throw it in the corner office. He came back cackling. "I hope it ruins her day."

Anthony and I went outside; Michael was on his way in. "We were just speaking of things generally offensive," I told him. "Oh, I didn't see Lenny out this weekend."

"Oh, you mean you haven't heard?" Michael announced triumphantly. I just looked at him.

"Tell us," Anthony prodded.

"Well," he said, "it seems she's been eighty-sixed from The Holy Spirit. *And* she's been eighty-sixed from the Monster and from Palladium."

"Wow," Anthony said. "That is truly amazing. I have never heard of anyone being kicked out of virtually every club in New York."

"Neither have I," I said. "What did they finally kick her out for?"

"Well," Michael began again, "it seems she went up to the d.j. booth one time too often and evidently Warren complained to the manager about it and when the night was over the manager came up to Lenny and told him he wasn't welcome there anymore."

"Well, thank God she's gone," I said. "You know, I was one of her last defenders in New York. I was one of the last people who would say something nice about her in public and she finally managed to offend even me. Last month, one Saturday night, she went up to Bobby Cantor and said to him, 'Oh, your friend what's-his-name is here.' Meaning me."

Anthony and Michael both looked at me. "Well, I can't remember what was so offensive about it at the time, but Bobby and I both agreed that it was gratuitously insulting and that Lenny had finally crossed that line even with us. And," I went on, "do you know that Lenny and I have the exact same birthday and it always falls around Columbus Day weekend and last year at the Columbus Day party he told me the d.j. was going to stop the music and wish him a happy birthday. I mean, she actually thought this was going to happen. The worst part, though, was how she would never remember that it was my birthday too."

"She was always that way," Michael said.

"Well, I'm glad she's gone," I said. "I can't believe it took so long. I'm twenty-seven and she's been around for as long as I can remember. She seems to remember things that predate me."

"I think she's older than that," Michael said.

"Do you really?" I asked.

"Oh, yes," he said. "I think she's at least thirty-eight or thirty-nine."

"That would make her particularly grotesque," Anthony said.

"Well," Michael said.

"Anyway," I said. "I'm glad she's gone, finally. I'm glad the social circuit finally took care of her.

As a matter of fact, I'd go so far as to say that the circuit owes us all something for having put up with her for so many years. I think we're due some sort of compensation for their collective passive poor judgment all this time."

"Well, come here," Michael said, producing a vial. "The circuit is going to reward you with a hit of K," he said knocking some into the cap. I leaned over with one finger against one nostril.

I decided to make this season's Closing Party my last time there. By this time many of the dealers had quit coming and some of them had gone out of business due to a decline in demand. Everyone I saw said hi and do you know where we can get drugs? "Honey, how nice to see you too," I finally said to Mark Brickman. "Why is everyone asking me this?"

He took his arms from around my waist but, pragmatically disenfranchised, he didn't give me attitude. "Well, only because I thought you might know, darling," he answered. I promised to tell him if I saw anyone.

I walked up the front stairs and stood in the stairwell and furtively snorted some K. I love furtiveness.

"Hah, Harold," Tom appeared.

"Well, hah, Tom," I said. "Should we do some K?"

"Well, sure," he said, and we climbed up the grey stairs. We found a spot and settled in. I handed Tom the bottle, then took it back to do some myself. "Look at this new way I learned to do K," I told him. I shook a little out into the cap and held it up to my nostril.

"Why, that's fabulous," Tom said. "That makes it a real aerosol."

My right nostril made a good snort.

Richard, the Queen of Caracas, came up the stairs. "Hello," he said in his clipped way. He stopped and blew his nose. "I was just going to do some K. Would you care to join me?"

"Thank you," I said. "We just did. Are you up to it, though, Richard? I remember the horrible scene of your nasal passages."

"My nasal passages are fine," he said, knocking some K out onto his fist. "They'll manage," he added, inhaling. Everything turned a muddy green and then became a design and then folded back. From the top of the space I saw Tom and Richard and me again on the stairs. I thought I was someone else tripping the video of my life.

"I'll be right back," Richard said. There was red and yellow light all around his head and his face was separated into little monochromes. "I have to get something," I think he said, and he skipped down the stairs.

"Where did Richard go?" I asked Tom. I was back in my body.

"He went to get something," he said. "Why?" Then Richard came back up.

"Let's make Richard disappear again," I said.

Richard disappeared and Tom laughed. "We made him disappear," he said.

"OK. Let's bring him back," I said, and we did.

Richard was unperturbed. "Come on," he said. "Let's do some ethyl."

I bunched up the corner of my T-shirt and Richard squirted it through. I put it in my mouth and it became nighttime and outdoors and I started seeing that concept again about how everything's the same as everything else and there's really no question and it looked like the numeral 3 the way it kept boinging back and connecting throughout time. It was a memory of a pleasure so intense it can't be remembered. And then with the velocity of the experience I went straight down.

If I wanted to leave The Holy Spirit dramatically, I guess I did, by passing out on the dance floor for the first time; OK, maybe the second. When I came to, Richard was holding me and we were sitting outside the dance floor.

Mark Brickman spotted us. "Darling," he exclaimed even more warmly than before. "I just wanted you to know, you can relax. I found drugs."

I looked up at the scene on the dance floor. "Where are we?" I asked.

"We're in The Holy Spirit," Richard said. "Are you OK?" He took his arms from around my shoulders.

"What night is this?" I asked, standing up.

"It's the Closing Party," he said, watching me.

I could remember arriving there for a Closing Party. But which one? "What year is this?" I asked.

"1985," Richard said.

Then the disco ball fell out of the ceiling, it just came loose and fell straight down and landed in the star machine. There was this big BOOM like a speaker blew and that was about it. Hardly anyone noticed. "Well," Mark Brickman said, "that's the Beginning of the End."

"Oh, please," Richard said. "If that was the Beginning of the End, it would have fallen and killed twenty people."

I just looked at them. 1985. I tried to place it. But the dream was over, and that was my last night at The Holy Spirit Dance Club.

Read to death
by a Japanese lesbian

A week later I heard from Himiko. I didn't ask how or why she got my number; hearing things around wasn't only inevitable, it was organized and efficient. I had only to remember the First Annual Christopher Street Liberation Day Ball, the night Bonds International Casino filled up with smoke and it was two hours before anyone realized it wasn't the smoke machine, it was an electrical fire. Four thousand people were calmly evacuated, but the next morning ten thousand of their friends knew about it before the rest of New York did.

I watched from my tenement doorway as Himiko's figure finally appeared in the top stairwell. "Sorry it took so long," she smiled. "I was looking for the elevator." She handed me flowers as she came in.

"I'm glad you called," I said. I put the three roses in a coffeepot, spreading them out in the water. I put it on the floor and we sat there on cushions, across from the window.

"Yes, well," she said, "I heard you were splitting after the Closing Party." She leaned back; she was wearing jeans, New Balance sneakers and a short sleeve sweatshirt.

"It was a weird night," I said. "I had like, a major trip."

"Do you follow astrology?" she asked me.

I shrugged while I rolled a joint.

"Astrologically, it was one of those nights," she said. "Several planets were in position."

"I wish someone would tell me about these things," I said. "I mean, in advance. They have this impact on me. Don't tell anyone, but I passed out on the dance floor."

"I won't tell anyone that," she said. "But what's this I hear about you not going to The Holy Spirit anymore."

I knew this was coming. The flowers were a definite indication, I was being set up. "It's over," I said casually, leaning forward and lighting the joint for her.

She just looked at me as she inhaled. She waited. "I mean," I went on, "I don't want to say anything negative if you had a good time, but come on, Himiko. You must've noticed that this party wasn't exactly a primitive ritual." She sputtered on the smoke when I said that. "I told you I haven't been having a good time. The scene's going downhill, I'm not happy about it, and I'm getting out," I said with finality.

"Boy, you seem a little angry," she said. The room was dim; it was early evening and the last grey light of the East Village was mixing black. Rooftops of other tenements settled in deep relief.

"Angry?" I asked, looking back at her. "OK, yeah," I said. "I'm angry. Who wouldn't be angry about what we've lost?

"Remember what it was like there?" I started. She nodded. "Remember how it was, every Saturday night we went to this major Club that no one else even knew about? I mean, you'd walk by the front of the building on your way in and you'd never even know from the outside what was going on in there. Remember what a secret it was?

165

"David Walken was telling this story one time, about how he was talking with some straight people who took a hit of ecstasy or something. He said, meanwhile he was probably higher than anyone on earth that weekend and these other people had no idea. I thought about it, for about a second. He probably really was higher than anyone on earth.

"Do you remember how it took up our whole weekend, and then we spent half the week recovering from it and the other half getting ready to do it again?"

"Yes," she said patiently.

"It gave us something to live for," I said. "I loved that Club. I do still love it but, gosh, Himiko, I don't want to become one of those people talking about the good old days, about how it used to be there. Maybe I was lucky enough to come by at the end of it, and maybe some of them are right and it's over...the ceremony's gone, and the Club's being opened to the public, to straight people."

"It *was* a ceremony," she agreed. She smiled and her eyes came over to me.

"A beautiful ceremony," I said. "With the d.j. as high priest and the music structured to introduce the evening, to lead us in, and then to start building up the energy. It got the whole primitive thing underway." We both laughed. "Then the ball would come down from the ceiling at the absolute peak. It would come down and the tree would rise up, and it was like the two units were coming together and meeting: a fertility ritual, a sexual act. I'm willing to believe that was a religious activity. And in any group of dancers that had a woman in it, like Diana or Mary, the

166

woman was the center. That looks like goddess worship to me.

"And then I thought about some other things, like how our dancing is such a basic expression of ourselves. It's just this movement that comes out of us, as naturally and directly as our hand-writing or our voices. Dancing is a worshipping before God," I said. I took a puff on the joint and choked on the smoke. "And everything in the Club was so ahead of the general culture: the music, the lighting and the sound technology, what we wore and how we talked. These were people who were the creators of culture; and you were either one of them, or one in-training. It was like a *convocation*.

"And so then the ball would come down, and think about it, we were actually worshiping this mirror disco ball, and we were all dancing and screaming as the energy was building about as high as it could. I felt like we were teasing, or playing with God somehow, seeing just how high we could crank it up. And then all of a sudden it broke each time: that was Sleaze, the relief music, the comedown.

"This was my religious education," I said. "This was my initiation, because whatever the night put me through, psychologically and emo-tionally, I had to get through it. Isn't that where terms like baptism and trial by fire come from—drug-induced initiations? I'm willing to believe that a structure of ritual as old as the planet probably has some validity.

"Then when I found myself among stars and asteroids, actually looking at them right next to me, well, I found out later that's called astral projection. And when I found myself looking down at the room from the ceiling, I know what that is too, it's out of body stuff. I came out of all this a stronger man, Himiko," I said. "That's what a religious initiation does, right?"

"You've sure changed in the year you've been there," she agreed. "Do you feel stronger?"

"Yeah, I do. That disco gave me strength and I'm grateful for it; I took it right from the energy I felt in the room. And when I learned just to get through the night, to get through every trip no matter what, I learned how to use that strength; I learned to direct it and control it.

"I found out something else too. If I didn't feel like dancing, all I had to do was go up to the dance floor and get the first step going. The energy would build up and take off from there, and I could use it to create anything I wanted. That's how I learned you can really do anything you want. That's a major thing, Himiko. That's power. That's creation."

"And all of that's just over now?" she asked me evenly.

"I'm not wasting my time there," I said. "And I'm not dancing with straight people."

"Maybe it's time now for straight people and gay people to dance together," Himiko shrugged. "Maybe that's why The Holy Spirit is changing now."

"You must be out of your mind," I said. "I have no intention of dancing with straight people, not now, not ever."

"Boy, are you hostile," she said.

"Yeah," I said. "I'm hostile. When I can forget about every horrible thing that straight people have ever done to me, I'll forget about being hostile." The leather string around my neck opened, and the picture of the white light that Himiko had given me on the dance floor slipped into my T-shirt. I was still pissed off. I just tied the string back.

"I think," she said with playful smugness, "that you're seeing present manifestations of past vibrations. If you've been reading, you know that every cause has an effect. And if we're seeing hard times at The Holy Spirit now, maybe that's the effect of past negative vibrations. Past," she repeated, looking at me. "Maybe now, in the present, we're being asked to use our own positive vibes to help The Holy Spirit through a difficult time."

I sat back, and blinked slowly. We didn't say anything, maybe for five minutes. Then: "Himiko," I said, "there's something else. Everything in nature exists in patterns and cycles, right? Maybe everyone else knew this kind of stuff before, but I never paid attention in science class and I never knew it until I danced. Then I saw that when I dance, I dance in a certain pattern. Then at some point the pattern changes and it grows into a new pattern. It repeats in a cycle."

Himiko looked at me as the distant sight of the moon brightened the room. She lit a cigarette and sat back.

"What I mean is," I said, "is that I honestly thought something was going to happen at The Holy Spirit Dance Club. And I still don't think I was wrong at the time. But now the indicators have changed: the energy level, not only at the Club but in New York too, has come down...

"Look, here's how it is: if The Holy Spirit Dance Club was the center of it all, or even if it wasn't, our social lives have changed profoundly recently. Going out is no longer a serious activity. Clubbing is not the big thing anymore, disco is over. The maturing of the baby boom has just about finished and as some people leave the club scene, there are fewer new ones coming in. And as the general population has gotten older, some people just quit going out. Why, I can't imagine.

"And let's face it, AIDS has done more than kill large numbers of people from the disco. Some people died, and a lot of the others got scared and some got depressed and started staying home. Some people stopped taking drugs for health reasons. A lot of the people who were out looking for sex quit.

"So everything has like, wound down, major. In many ways it's affected all of New York; you can see it in the energy level in the air. Who ever thought New York would have chain discos from out-of-town? Those aren't clubs, they're bars out of control. And there are actually fast food chains on Fifth Avenue, and Broadway has never had fewer shows playing. Things are boring here. But I don't think that means it's over. If there's a cycle, then maybe this is just a refractory period. A couple of minutes of rest before something even bigger than anything we ever expected at The Holy Spirit happens and happens like, big time. I used to think it would be the end of the world, but now I don't. Now I think it'll be something just as big, but fabulous instead."

"I wasn't sure how sensitive you were to these things," she said. "I think something's going to happen on the planet soon too."

"So don't you think we have a responsibility to that?" I asked. "I mean, I don't know how we're

170

supposed to do this, but we can't stay in this Club; we have to go out and find out where it's happening next. Except we don't know where it's going to be happening this time. We don't even know what it'll look like; maybe it won't even be dancing this time, who knows. But it will be somewhere, and we have to go out and keep it going.

"We have to get out of the Club, Himiko. I'm seeing things that are frightening me: gay men in wing tip shoes. Maybe there are a lot of them, even. Maybe I have less in common with other gay people than I thought. I grew up thinking that every gay person wanted to live the disco life; now I realize that only some of us wanted to, or only some of us wanted to to this extent.

"I'm seeing well-dressed, good-looking hetero men. Not that that's frightening, exactly, but it certainly shakes some of my premises. When I joined the circuit, being gay was the big thing and everyone admitted that gay people did it better. We were better dressed and had better taste, we were artistic and creative, we were better looking, better groomed, and pumped up. Fashion started here and so did style.

"Well, not any more. A lot of those fashionable gay people are dead and a lot of the rest are depressed; their not dancing is only an indication of that. They've given up the lead in every area. And that affects the disco, too. The recording industry used to market a record by pushing it to the gay d.j.'s, and the songs we liked in the clubs were the ones that became the big sellers. Now the recording industry markets a record through MTV, and we're left listening to the Top 40."

"What did you think," she interrupted me, sitting up. Her bangs fell across her forehead. "That we were some kind of chosen people?"

"Well, yeah. I did. We sure looked chosen."

"Harold," she said, pushing her hair back, "all people are God's chosen people. If unification is a goal, how can separatism be a means?"

"I don't know," I said. "I'm very confused now. All my premises are upside down. Maybe you're right. You must be right. I don't know."

"Harold," she said again, "what you're saying is that the group we joined on the party circuit no longer exists. And you're saying that AIDS has changed our lives in many ways. But maybe one reason for this tragedy is to bring about something greater."

"Like what, in the short term?"

"Like I don't know," she said. "But whatever's happened has happened already. If there are fewer gay people in the Club and you're seeing for the first time gay people who live in the regular society, maybe assimilation has already occurred and we have to catch up."

"Right," I said. "I'll buy that. And that's why we can't stay in the Club any longer. It's time to come out for air, or we'll end up like people who talk about the good old days and get stuck in a time warp. Did you hear me before, doing it? I almost came very close to taking a unique experience and performing the very un-unique act of getting caught in the past. It's time for us to come out of the Club and join everyone else. Find out where the energy concentration is going to be next and bring what we've learned there."

"You mean you think we should all go out and start our own clubs."

172

"Something like that."

"Maybe we can have a home base?" she suggested. "There's no other dance club like The Holy Spirit. You said The Holy Spirit is a special place, that something was getting ready to happen there. If that's true, how could it be different now?"

I looked at her silently. "The people there are special too," she said. "You said so yourself, they're creators of energy, forces within the culture. There are huge amounts of artistry, talent and energy in that Club, Harold. You know about energy. And if something's going to happen, we need to keep these people involved.

"Everyone who went into that Club came out better for it. Richard is designing lighting in Rome. Diana's a successful promoter. I see ads David Walken designs all over town. And who's your other friend, what's his name, he's been around forever, he has a very physical presence."

"Robert."

"Robert. He used to be a clerk on Wall Street and now he's some kind of manager or something. And that strange doctor, he seems bright, even if he's a little weird.

"I agree, when things started going wrong at the Club, maybe management didn't make the best decisions, or maybe their primary concern was financial. But they built the place and we should be grateful. The Holy Spirit Dance Club can be a palace of art, Harold, and a whole planet of art could grow outward from there. And that's only one idea. One possible interpretation of what's going on.

"And there's something else you should consider too, Harold. To change something, all you have to do is change your mind about it. You can make something you dislike something you like.

"Maybe it *is* time for straight people and gay people to dance in the same Club. Maybe when you get rid of your hostility, you can find a way to help The Holy Spirit through all this. A lot of people have already given up," she went on. "They went to The Holy Spirit looking for something fashionable. Or something intellectual. We have to help the Club."

The joint was burned down; I dropped it into the ashtray. "Anyway, Himiko," I said, "I *can't* go back. I already told everyone I was cleaning out my locker and never going back there again."

"I think," she said, looking at me, her black eyes deep and bright, "that people will be glad to see you on the dance floor." There was a soft, rushing sound. I looked over at the roses she'd brought me and they were opening; their petals were spreading, making a noise. "Wake up, Harold," she said. "You know you'll succeed."

I glanced at the flowers again. I felt like I'd been spoken to by the Universe.

The last song before the queens straggle down the stairs

And then I figured I was being too political about the whole thing anyway. I still don't know what to do, or what the next step is.

Just keep dancing, I guess.

ABOUT THE AUTHOR

Joseph Puccia was born in Brooklyn.
This is his first novel.